VENGEANCE
IS FOREVER

Robert Fisher

Vengeance is Forever Robert Fisher
Copyright © 2022 La Maison Publishing
ISBN: 978-1-970153-43-9
Distribution: Ingram Book Company

Cover Art by Aaron Williams

Maison

La Maison Publishing
Vero Beach, Florida
The Hibiscus City
lamaisonpublishing@gmail.com

Chapter 1
The Gilded Cage

To anyone else, living in a secluded lakefront mansion surrounded by the snow covered majesty of the Japanese Alps would be a great vacation. However, to Mai Yunao it felt like a prison. She sat on the couch in the large ornate living room of her father's secluded mansion, looking out at the lake and the mountains beyond. She had been there for almost four weeks, being watched at all times by the Triad soldiers ordered by her father to protect her at all costs, until it was safe for her to leave. What was most infuriating though was that she couldn't walk outside without one or two guards following her.

She tried to keep herself busy, however she could. She would read from one of the many books in the mansions library. She would paint the landscapes but that got boring so for the most part she either read or watched movies. While she did spend her time catching up on shows and movies that she missed, she watched the news the most. It felt cathartic to be reminded of the world from her million dollar prison. She turned away from the window, picked the TV remote off the coffee table and turned on the TV. She flipped through the channels absent-mindedly doing it more out of boredom.

The guards were instructed to give her anything she wanted to make her stay as pleasant as possible, but she couldn't really think of anything that she wanted. She continued clicking through channels, eventually stopping on a movie channel. The movie it was showing was an old action movie that she'd never seen before. Ordinarily she would have skipped it since she despised action movies preferring documentaries instead. Just by looking at the images on the screen it looked like it had a low budget and a cheap plot. She was about to change the channel but decided to look up the title out of curiosity.

Mai stopped when she read the title: Escape from New York (1981) with Kurt

Russell and Adrienne Barbeau. As she read the title and the movie summary she remembered hearing about it several months ago. She continued watching the movie, not really paying attention to it. Just then the main character of the movie appeared on screen. He had shoulder-length brown hair and a black eye patch. He reminded her of the man who told her about the movie.

A man she initially regarded as a brainless trigger happy thug. However, after spending some time with him she realized she was wrong and began to develop feelings for the man. It had been four weeks since she had last seen him. Her father had hired him to rescue her from a rival criminal organization and protect her from a greater enemy. The last time she saw him was on Sankan Island, an island ruled by criminals and ignored by the rest of the world. She didn't even know if he was still alive, though she hoped he was.

Mai continued watching the movie; admittedly it did look interesting if not completely unrealistic. *Why would America convert New York into a prison in the first place?* Mai asked herself as she watched the movie.

She wondered if he liked it because of the action or because he related to the main character since they had both lost an eye and covered it with an eye patch. Just then she knew what the guards could bring her, but she shrugged knowing that contact with him was against their orders. Still, she thought, it would be nice to hear from Simon Kane again.

Chapter 2
Declaration of War

The Neutral Executive for Total World Order Regardless of Consequence, commonly referred to as the Networc, consisted of eight multinational corporations with various specialties that served as the Networc's branches. The CEO's of these corporations, each referred to by a number, made up the Networc's ruling board of directors. Only one of the eight board members knew the identities of the other seven board members for security reasons. Known as Mr. Zero, he was the CEO of the Swiss manufacturing firm known as Kronos International. Through various legal and illegal methods the Networc had secretly manipulated the course of the world's governments since the organization's inception.

Mr. Zero sat at his desk, he was a tall, handsome, well-built, younger man of pale complexion with blonde hair. He looked out at the resort town of St. Moritz. Even though it was night, the village seemed to glow in the dark under a blanket of soft snow. Beyond the village was Lake St. Moritz, frozen and covered in snow. Looming above were the snowcapped mountains of the Swiss Alps. His mansion overlooked the Swiss resort town. At times he felt like a medieval king surveying his kingdom when he looked out at St. Moritz from his office window; however, he was more than a king and now was not the time for study.

He turned away from his window to the laptop on his desk. On the screen were seven boxes each with a hidden face in them. Under each box were the names of the individual board members of the Networc. On their screens the various board members saw the same thing on their screens, though on the top of their screens was a box for Mr. Zero. The Board of Directors always teleconferenced via scrambled transmission. Meetings like this usually involved status updates on the

Networcs various projects. This meeting, however, was different as it had to do with a certain foe of the Networc.

Mr. Zero smiled upon seeing that his fellow board members were all in attendance. "Gentlemen, shall we begin?"

They all responded yes, their voices scrambled into a robotic growl by the computers.

"Now then, we are to discuss a solution to the Simon Kane situation," said Mr. Zero.

"Sir, we know he is working with the Heise She Li Triad," said Mr. Seven, the CEO of the Networcs global communications branch known to the world as Minute Broadcasting.

Mr. Zero was not surprised since the Heise She Li Triad was the Networcs largest rival. "Yes, I recall you telling me that, but do you have a point?"

"Yes, if we could find out where Kane and these people the Triad recruited are based then perhaps we could deploy the Upper Echelon to liquidate them," said Mr. Seven.

The Upper Echelon served as the Networcs intelligence and covert ops branch.

Its operatives referred to as Counselors. "That is true, but where are these people based?" asked Mr. Zero.

"We suspect it's the Triad's outpost on Sankan Island," said Mr. One, CEO of the global PMC known as Applied Dynamics which served as the Networcs military and intelligence branch.

"I see, and how sure are you of this?" asked Mr. Zero.

"One hundred percent sure. After they attacked VULCAN base, I instructed the Upper Echelon to keep Sankan Island under heavy surveillance," Mr. One answered. "Recently we spotted them arriving there by plane"

Mr. Zero thought for a minute. "Mr. One I want you to send the Upper Echelon to attack every major Triad facility on Earth," said Mr. Zero. "I also want you to send a Lower Echelon strike force to the Triads outpost on Sankan"

"Their orders are to attack the Triads tower, kill Simon Kane and generally do as much damage as possible," he continued. While the Networcs military, known as the

Lower Echelon, was capable of such an operation the other board members were surprised by the request and perplexed by it.

"Pardon me sir, but is one man really worth that much effort and why attack the Triad as a whole?" asked Mr. Five, CEO of the global bank known as King Midas Holdings, which served as the Networcs financial branch.

"Shall I remind you all of this man's actions against us?" asked Mr. Zero.

Hearing no objections, Mr. Zero took a deep breath. "Eight months ago this man's actions resulted in the failure of Project: BIG PICTURE. Four weeks ago he caused Project: MOSES to fail and finally two weeks ago he and several others did the same to Project: GHOST FIRE."

He could imagine that at this moment Mr. One and Mr. Two were squirming nervously since he had chosen them to oversee Project: MOSES and Project GHOST FIRE, respectively.

Mr. Zero paused for a few seconds to let his words sink in. "Three times in one year this man has involved himself in our affairs, I assure you there will not be a fourth. Are we in agreement?"

Again the other six board members responded with various forms of yes.

"While you have a point, this is not just about the Kane problem it is also about sending a message to the Triad," answered Mr. Zero.

"Be that as it may, I am concerned that such an action would not only be a drain on our resources but also serve to plunge us into another drain on our resources," continued Mr. Five.

"He attacked us first, you cowardly swine!" Mr. One barked.

"One man does not justify deploying the Lower Echelon!" replied Mr. Five.

"Enough!" yelled Mr. Zero, annoyed at the Boards bickering. "In the past we would merely ignore such a problem or deploy a Counselor to deal with him."

"For too long Simon Kane and the Triad have been a thorn in our side and it is time we dealt with them...harshly," said Mr. Zero. "Mr. One, I also want you to deploy

Counselors Stenz and Benton to find and kidnap Mai Yunao."

"Why? She's nothing to us?" asked Mr. One.

"True, but she is something to the Triad's leader and she could provide us with some leverage over him," replied Mr. Zero. "Once they have her, tell them to bring her to TREADWATER, keep me updated of the situation Mr. One."

"Now then, this meeting is over," said Mr. Zero as he pressed a button on the laptop that terminated the transmission.

Suddenly there was a knock on the door, "come in," he said.

Mr. Zero looked up to the door just as his two personal assistants and personal bodyguards, Hai and Lo Nguyen, walked inside. They were identical twin sisters he had adopted from Vietnam. Both of them had the same short black hair with bangs in the front as well as the same attractive figure. The only way to tell them apart was how they dressed. Hai wore a long sleeveless black dress with a red seam and red heels.

Her sister, Lo wore a long identical red dress with a black seam and black heels. Mr. Zero referred to them by their first names mainly because he liked how it sounded. They followed him wherever he went using their skills to both protect and assist him wherever he went.

"What is it ladies?" asked Mister Zero.

"We have reservations at La Marmite with the Swiss Air Force colonels in an hour," said Miss Lo.

"Ah yes, of course, Miss Lo bring the car around and Miss Hai please get my suitcase," said Mr. Zero.

"Yes sir," Miss Hai replied.

Miss Hai and Miss Lo turned and walked out of the office. Mr. Zero stood up and walked to his bedroom and got dressed for his meeting. As he got dressed he didn't think about the conversation, secure that the next time he heard from Mr. One two of the greatest threats to the Networc would be eliminated.

Chapter 3
Revenge of the Evil Empire

"Dude, I'm telling you, Return of the Jedi, is the best Star Wars movie" said Mack.

"No, The Force Awakens is the best" protested Dennis.

Mack Roycewicz and Dennis Faraday sat arguing in the small library in the Triad's building on Sankan island. Located in the Devils Sea, Sankan Island was a hub of criminal activity that was divided in half by the Heise She Li Triad and the Vasilev Syndicate.

"The Force Awakens doesn't count," Mack replied.

Mack Roycewicz, a former Army Ranger turned international assassin, was a tall muscular man dressed in a red and green Hawaiian shirt and khakis who served as the team's sharpshooter. Dennis straightened his glasses; he was an average looking man, wearing gray pants and a white dress shirt with a black tie. He served as the team's computer specialist.

"What do you mean the Force Awakens doesn't count?" inquired Dennis.

"It's the same as a New Hope, besides Rey is a broken character." Mack replied.

Seated across from them reading a Bible was the team's hand-to-hand combat specialist, a former IRA terrorist turned Catholic Nun named Siobhan Costello. She was dressed in the black and white habit of a Catholic nun. Half asleep in a chair next to Siobhan was the team's mechanic and sniper, an ex-CIA agent named Deon Bowman. He was wearing a dark yellow short-sleeve shirt and black urban camo pants.

"Okay you're right about Rey, but how is it the same as New Hope?" Dennis asked.

"Dude, did you even see the movie? It's the same plot, the same characters, they may as well have called it Star Wars: A Newer Hope," said Mack.

Deon laughed softly, "good one," he mumbled having been rousted from sleep by the argument.

"See even the jarhead agrees with me," said Mack.

"That's not what he said," Dennis pointed out.

"Either way, I'm taking it as a win," said Mack smugly.

"Excuse me what are you talking about?" Siobhan asked innocently.

"Star Wars, you know, Luke Skywalker? Han Solo? The Force?" answered Dennis confused by her response.

"Oh...I've never seen it, sorry," replied Siobhan as she resumed reading.

Dennis, Mack and Deon looked at her stunned by her answer. Before any of them could respond, a familiar voice buzzed over the intercom telling them to go to the meeting room in the basement. They got up and walked out of the library. The three of them took the elevator to the meeting room located on one of the several sublevels located beneath the building. The meeting room was a large rectangular room with a wooden boardroom table in the middle and a screen on the far wall.

Waiting for them was the head of the Triads operations on Sankan, an enigmatic Chinese man named Deng Shen. Deng was wearing a white dress shirt, black tie, black trench coat and black pants. Next to him, was the leader of the team, a former SEAL team six operator turned black-ops CIA agent named Simon Kane. He was a tall well-built rugged looking man with black slicked back hair. He wore a black shirt and dark green pants with a dark blue trench coat.

Over his right eye was a black eye patch to cover up the loss of his right eye. Simon, Mack, Dennis, Deon and Siobhan had all been recruited by the Triad to help bring down the Triads greatest enemy: the Networc. Simon used to belong to a covert branch of the CIA known as Silhouette; he joined the Triad after a Networc agent killed his wife. He brought along his friend from Silhouette: Deon Bowman. Mack and Dennis were recruited to the Triad's team after the Calabrese crime family put a hit on them.

Siobhan Costello, a former member of the IRA, was recruited after Deng had convinced her that she could atone for her sins as a terrorist by destroying the Networc.

"My God, it's the trench coat mafia," said Mack sarcastically as they walked in and took their seats.

"You done?" asked Simon sardonically.

"Not really, I have ten more minutes of material," replied Mack sarcastically.

"We don't have ten minutes," Deng replied.

"Damn, because I had few good ones," said Mack.

"I think we'll manage, now that we're all here, I'll begin" said Simon. "It has been two weeks since we attacked the Networcs lab in Iceland."

"And so far we have heard nothing from them," Deng interrupted.

"Why is that so surprising, hell it's only been two weeks," said Mack.

"True, but we've been keeping a close eye on Prometheus Technologies ever since and so far we haven't seen or heard anything out of the ordinary," answered Deng.

"Any word on Sasha?" Deon asked.

"None," replied Deng.

"Good," Deon muttered.

"Though we've analyzed the file she gave us and we have a lead," said Simon.

"She believes that if we find one of these Counselors that they can lead us to the Networc," Deng explained.

"Great when do we leave?" Mack asked.

"Not for a little while," said Deng.

"That brings me to our next issue. The lack of any activity from the Networc tells me that they are planning something big," said Simon. "I don't know what it is exactly but Deng tells me we need to prepare for the worst."

"Indeed, I've placed sentries all over our part of the island and I've notified our neighbors across the street," said Deng, casually referring to the Russian Mafia organization known as the Vasilev Syndicate. "However, as a security measure I am placing the building under full lockdown, which in layman's terms means no one goes in or out for the next two weeks."

"Now then, anyone else got something to say?" asked Simon.

"Uh yeah, Siobhan's never seen Star Wars," said Mack.

The five men looked at her surprised.

"That's just wrong," said Simon dryly with a shrug.

Chapter 4

Fox In The Hen House

Mai Yunao prepared herself for going to sleep. She looked out the bedroom at the mountains in the distance one final time before she lay down on the bed. Outside, her security guards were patrolling the perimeter of the mansion. She placed her glasses on the nightstand beside her bed and slowly drifted off to sleep. Mai's father had assigned seven Triad commandos to guard Mai at the mansion.

They were each armed with a submachine gun and an automatic pistol. The men patrolled the grounds relentlessly. They were positive that an attack would come from land since the only way into the compound was the front gate. For months, the Networc had known where Mai was being hidden, however, they chose not to act on it deeming it irrelevant until now. Counselor Stenz and Counselor Benton were not told why they had to kidnap her nor did they ask.

Mr. One had shown them a blueprint of the facility and explained how they would enter. They would parachute out of a plane at night, enter the mansion, capture Mai and destroy the mansion. It had been fifteen minutes since they had jumped out of the plane; they landed in a clearing on the mansions grounds. They hid their parachutes and cocked their rifles. They were dressed in the standard outfit befitting members of the Networcs Upper Echelon: black dress shirt and tie, black pants with a gray belt, black trench coat, gray gloves and a black fedora with a wide brim and a gray band.

They carried silenced XM8 assault rifles, the standard issue assault rifle for Counselors, and their standard issue sidearm: a Glock 19 with a suppressor. Slowly they made their way through the small forest till they could see the mansion. In front of them walked a guard, Counselor Stenz pulled out his knife and jumped out from behind the guard. Quickly, he placed his right hand over the guard's mouth while he slid the knife into the guard's back.

He looked back at Counselor Benton, the two men nodded and began slowly approaching the mansion. They had approached the front door when it began to open; Counselor Stenz fired four rounds at the door. On the other side they heard the thud of a body hitting the floor. They opened the door and walked into the living room of the mansion, stepping over the dead body of the guard. Silently they entered the bedroom and opened the door.

Quietly, on the bed fast asleep was Mai. Benton and Stenz smiled like hunters having just sighted their prey. Counselor Stenz placed his gloved hand roughly over Mai's mouth.

Instantly she awoke. She tried to scream but her protests were muffled by the gloved hand. As she struggled, Counselor Benton reached into his pocket and pulled out a small syringe and injected it in her neck. He pressed down on the plunger and slowly Mai lapsed into unconsciousness. Counselor Benton placed his hand on the communicator in his ear.

"We have Lotus, send the extraction team now," said Benton.

"Roger," replied a voice on the other side of the communicator.

Benton and Stenz carried Mai's unconscious body out to the back porch of the mansion. In the distance they could hear the approaching sound of a helicopter. As they waited anxiously for the helicopter to approach, they heard footsteps behind them. They turned around and saw six guards running toward them with their guns drawn.

Stenz and Benton aimed there rifles at the guards and swiftly fired at them each with one bullet to the head of each guard. Once the guards had been dispatched they looked up and saw their helicopter. It was a modified UH-72 Lakota helicopter; they had added a hidden single shot missile launcher below the cockpit simply for this mission. The chopper landed and they quickly got in. They strapped Mai and themselves in and closed the door.

Swiftly, the chopper began to rise up into the air.

"Torch it," said Benton.

The pilot nodded and pressed the red button on the stick. Instantly, a missile streaked forward from the helicopter towards the mansion and exploded in a hellish fireball. The fire spread outward until it consumed the mansion. As the chopper turned and flew away, Counselor Stenz pressed his earpiece communicator.

"Mr. One, we have Lotus and the garden is on fire," said Counselor Stenz.

"Understood," replied the electronically scrambled voice of Mr. One.

Thousands of miles away on the top floor of the headquarters of Applied Dynamics in Johannesburg South Africa, Mr. One hung up on Counselor Stenz. They would take her to one of the Networcs most secure facilities known as TREADWATER. Mr. One turned to his computer and composed an E-mail reading:

Proceed with attack.

He sent the message to a unit of Lower Echelon commandos that he had tasked with attacking the Triads Sankan headquarters.

He leaned back in his chair, "the fools have no idea what's coming," muttered Mr. One, a sadistic smile crossing his face.

Chapter 5

Home Invasion

For the last two days, since the meeting, the Triad building had been completely sealed off. Those inside tried to occupy their time as best they could. While Deng and the rest of the Triad had many tasks that demanded their attention, Simon, Deon, Siobhan Mack and Dennis had no pressing matters to attend to. Normally Siobhan would be working at a soup kitchen aiding the destitute residents of the island. Mack and Dennis would usually be in the library or playing video games while Simon and Deon would be in the underground shooting range.

They were all waiting for word from Deng for any news on the Networc. Despite the lockdown they had settled into a routine. Since Siobhan couldn't leave for the soup kitchen she spent most of her time either in the library reading or in her room praying. The day-to-day activities of the others were mostly unaffected by the lockdown. At the moment, Simon and Deon were asleep in their rooms while Mack and Dennis were in the library.

Down the hall from Simon and Deon's room was Siobhan's room where she was inside praying.

"I'm telling you, Darth Vader would totally beat Darth Maul in a fight" Mack argued as he and Dennis walked to the library one floor below.

"You're wrong, Maul would win," replied Dennis.

"Why, because he has that double-edged light saber?" inquired Mack sarcastically.

"Look we've been arguing about this all day, they wouldn't fight in the first place because they existed at different times," responded Dennis.

"That's such a cop out man, just go with the spirit of the question," said Mack.

"It's not even a question, it's a what-if scenario," protested Dennis.

Suddenly before either of them could respond the building shook followed instantly by a loud explosion from above. The explosion was followed by the chattering of helicopters outside. The two men were knocked onto the floor by the explosion and the shaking.

"What was that?!" yelled Dennis as he picked up his glasses and tried to stand up.

"Not a what-if scenario," said Mack dryly.

Before they could say or do anything they heard muffled automatic fire coming from the floors above them. "That's not good" said Mack as he pulled out his pistol, a Tanfoglio T95 Combat.

"Let's go," said Mack as he turned to run towards the stairwell at the end of the hall.

"Go? what do you mean go?" asked Dennis as he straightened his glasses.

"Where the fuck do you think?" asked Mack as he ran toward the stairwell.

Dennis shrugged and drew his pistol, a Sig Sauer P230, despite the fact that he barely knew how to use it.

Simon was rousted from sleep as soon as he heard the explosion. He jumped out of bed and reached for his shoulder holster. Suddenly a large armor clad figure crashed through his window, aiming a rifle at him. The man had rappelled down from the roof since Simon could see his tether. Simon kicked the man in the chest knocking the rifle out of his hands and sending him backward.

The man responded by pulling out a knife and smiling arrogantly. Luckily, Simon had his wrist blade since he never slept without it. It was a metal armband around his wrist with a knife that popped out via a spring mechanism. Simon flicked his wrist back and out popped the knife, it wasn't as big as the other man's knife but it was all Simon had since he couldn't get to his pistol. The man lunged at him with the knife, Simon deflected it with his wrist blade.

The two men stood, pushing their blades against each other, struggling against each other's strength. With his free hand, Simon struck the man in his face knocking him off his balance. Sensing an opportunity, Simon grabbed the tether and wrapped it around the man's neck. Finally, Simon threw him out the window causing him to be strangled by his own rappelling cord.

"You should have knocked," muttered Simon as he slid the knife back into the armband.

He quickly put on his shoulder holster followed by his dark blue trench coat. He looked down at the rifle on the ground; it was a Heckler and Koch G36C assault rifle. Simon picked it up and checked to see if it had a full mag. He shrugged and cocked the rifle. Outside in the hall, Simon heard gun fire; he opened the door and saw Siobhan, dressed in her black and white habit, running towards three men dressed just like the man that had attacked him.

The three, black clad soldiers, surrounded her like wild animals surrounding their prey. With almost supernatural speed she smashed one of the soldier's feet with her foot and yanked his rifle out of the soldier's hands. Finally, she turned it around and fired one shot at the man's head killing him instantly. She turned around and tossed the gun at one of the soldiers knocking him on the ground.

While the other man was trying to get up Siobhan grabbed the other soldier and hit him in the neck with the side of her hand. Finally, she smashed his head into the wall making a painful cracking sound. Before letting him go she pulled his knife out of his belt. She spun around and brought the knife down into his chest. As the man gasped for breath she leaned in close to him.

"You will be welcomed into the kingdom of heaven, free of your sins," whispered Siobhan calmly.

The man whose head she just slammed into the wall slowly began to rise up behind her holding a pistol groggily. Siobhan sighed; she jumped up and in one move stabbed the man in his neck causing him to fall on the floor, blood spilling out of his neck. Siobhan could tell that eyes were watching her. She turned around and saw Simon and Deon staring at her both impressed and mostly stunned at what they had just witnessed. Siobhan waved her hand and smiled at them.

"Hello," said Siobhan politely.

"Damn" grunted Deon.

"That's putting it mildly," replied Simon.

Before anyone could say anything Deon and Mack ran into the hallway from the stairwell entrance in the other side of the hallway.

"Guys, are you...holy shit," said Mack upon seeing the three dead bodies on the floor.

"Who?" asked Dennis.

"Who do you think?" said Simon pointing to Siobhan.

"Hi Mack. Hi Dennis," said Siobhan warmly.

"Yo," said Mack.

Dennis tried not to vomit at the grisly sight in front of him. Suddenly another explosion rocked the building.

"We should get going" said Siobhan as she picked up one of the soldiers rifles, an H&K 416.

She cocked the rifle and ran to the stairwell at the other end of the hallway.

"I am really glad she's on our side," muttered Deon.

"You aren't the only one," Simon replied.

They followed Siobhan up the stairwell ready for anything. Before following them into the stairwell Simon looked at the bodies of the dead men. They were dressed in all black combat gear, their faces covered in black masks. Simon noticed that they were devoid of any markings or identification, which gave him some idea as to who had sent these men.

He shrugged, deciding instead to deal with the attackers and investigate later. Simon turned and followed the others up the stairwell.

Chapter 6

When The Ants Go Marching In...

As they ran up the stairwell the gunfire and helicopter engines got louder and louder. Upon exiting the stairwell they saw four Triad commandos running down the hall. Simon grabbed one of them and asked what was going on.

"We're going to get Mr. Shen! Follow us," yelled the man.

Simon, Siobhan, Dennis, Mack and Deon followed the man into the garden on the roof of the building. Next to the garden was a large red structure with three floors and a red pagoda atop it, a structure which served as Deng's private residence. Smoke bellowed forth from a hole on the second floor of the building. They could hear echoes of gunfire emanating from the top floor of the building.

"Who the hell are these guys?" asked Mack as they followed the Triad commandos into the building.

"I've seen them before," said Simon dismissively.

Before Mack or the others could respond they arrived at Deng's office. Lying on the floor outside the door to his office were two dead soldiers. Simon, Deon, Siobhan, Mack, Dennis and the Triad commandos ran into the office. There was a hole in the wall the size of a car and part of his bookcase was on fire. Propped up against the wall on the other side of the office was Deng on the floor.

His clothes were shredded and burned, the left side of his head was covered in blood. In his left hand was his pistol, a QSZ-92. As they walked in he raised his head up at them weakly and smiled.

"Are you alright?" asked Dennis.

Deng looked at him annoyed, "Better than them," he said gesturing to the dead soldiers.

"Where's Mazin?" Mack asked.

"Dead, we were having a meeting when these assholes attacked," said Deng. He pointed to the dead body of his personal assistant on the other side of the room.

"Sir, we have to get you out of here immediately," said one of the Triads commandos.

"Right, activate Cat Scratch Protocol," said Deng, the soldier nodded and pulled out his cellphone. Deng dialed a number and began speaking in Cantonese.

"Hold on before you activate...whatever the hell Cat Scratch Protocol is we have to get rid of those helicopters first," said Simon.

As if in answer, one of the helicopters hovered outside the hole in the office. They stared at it transfixed as the pilot prepared to fire at them. They could see the pilot through the dark tinted windows.

"Screw it" muttered Simon.

Simon aimed his pistol at the pilots head and fired five shots at him. Three of the bullets hit the man in the head, the other two hit him in the neck, instantly killing him. The helicopter gyrated chaotically before crashing on the edge of the garden below and exploding. The force of the blast knocked everyone backward.

"Huh, I didn't think that would work," observed Simon.

"First time I ever saw someone take out a helicopter with a pistol," said Deon.

"First time for everything," said Simon dismissively.

"Sir, Flying Fish is inbound," said the Triad commando as he returned his phone to his pocket.

"Good, by the time we get downstairs they should be there," said Deng as two of the Triad commandos helped him up.

"Hold on, what about the other helicopter?" asked Mack.

"We'll, deal with that shit when we get to it," said Simon as they ran out of the office with Deng.

"Well guys' let's get funky," said Mack.

*****

At that moment in Sankan harbor the head of the Flying Fish Trading Company walked out of his office having just received a phone call from the Triad. His name was Ben Martin, a tall black man dressed in a black t-shirt, pants and a green camo jacket. Before walking out of his office he put on his reflective aviator sunglasses. The other two members the Flying Fish Trading company were a Cuban American woman named Fiona Ramos and a Japanese American man named Kenji Yamada, both of them wanted criminals.

Fiona possessed a busty hour glass figure with a light brown skin tone. She wore a white-short sleeved crop top and skintight blue jean short shorts with a leather brown double vertical shoulder holster that held her two Smith and Wesson 645 pistols, affectionately dubbed Bart and Lisa. Kenji, a well-exercised Japanese man had short spiky black hair, a long-sleeve dark red shirt and black camo pants.

The Flying Fish Trading company typically was hired by either the Vasilev Syndicate or the Triad to smuggle illicit materials to and from Sankan. While Kenji served as the teams sniper, Fiona was the team's weapons specialist. Ben's specialty was hand-to-hand combat and maintaining the Rumrunner, the teams modified Grumman HU-16 Albatross seaplane. However, unknown to everyone on the island, they were actually members of a secret organization within the CIA known as Silhouette. Kenji and Fiona had been released from prison and sent to Sankan to spy on the Triad and Vasilev Syndicate under the guidance of Silhouette agent, Ben Martin.

Occasionally, they would be contacted by Silhouettes Director with certain missions to carry out in the region. Currently, they were keeping a particular eye on the former Silhouette agents Simon Kane and Deon Bowman and reporting back to Silhouette. At the moment, Fiona and Kenji were outside watching the attack on the Triads building in the distance.

"Damn!" said Fiona as she watched the other helicopter flying in circles around the building like vultures surrounding their prey.

"I wonder who destroyed the other chopper," Kenji asked.

"Who gives a shit, I just wish I was in the middle of that fight, give Bart and Lisa a chance to lay down the law," said Fiona tapping the butt of one of her pistols.

"Careful, what you wish for," said Kenji smugly.

"Fuck that I want to have some fun," said Fiona.

Before either of them could say anything else Ben walked out of the building and walked up to them carrying an M72 LAW missile launcher in his right hand.

"We've got a job," said Ben.

"Go on," asked Kenji.

"Deng activated Cat Scratch Protocol," answered Ben.

"Jobs simple: we go in, get Deng and his people out and drive them to the airport," answered Ben.

"I only have one question: Who gets to fire the LAW?" asked Fiona.

"You," said Ben as he tossed her the LAW rocket launcher.

She caught it in her left hand and checked it. "Ahhh Mi amour," said Fiona as she studied the weapon and slung it over her shoulder casually.

"Nothing for me," asked Kenji dryly.

"Go inside and grab the AK, but hurry, we are leaving in five," said Ben.

Kenji shrugged, annoyed at not being able to use his sniper rifle. Regardless he ran inside and returned shortly with an Ak-74u submachine gun. When he returned Fiona and Ben were already in the truck.

"Come on slowpoke," yelled Fiona tauntingly over the roar of the trucks engine.

Kenji sat in the front next to Ben while Fiona sat in the back.

"Let's rock and roll bitches," said Fiona as she put on her goggles.

Ben shifted gears and the truck lurched forward and they headed to the Triads building.

Chapter 7

All to Pieces

By the time Simon, Siobhan, Dennis, Mack and Deon had arrived at the lobby Deng had lost consciousness. His arms were on Deon and Dennis's shoulder while Simon, Mack, Siobhan and four Triad commandos guarded him.

"Is he still alive?" asked Mack glancing at him.

Siobhan checked his pulse, "he needs help quickly!"

"I was afraid of that" grunted Simon.

"It's your call MONOLITH what do we do?" asked Deon referring to Simon by his codename from when they were in Silhouette.

"Only thing we can do is get him to the airport," said Simon.

Simon looked over to the Triad commandos. "We'll stay here with him, you guys go out and see if our ride is here!"

The four guards looked at each other wondering if they should be taking orders from him. They looked back at him. "Don't worry, we'll take care of him trust me," said Simon.

The commandos nodded and ran outside to wait for their pickup while Simon rejoined the others.

As soon as the guards made it outside they were mowed down by a hail of heavy machine gun fire from above. Simon turned just in time to see them fall to the ground dead. The helicopter hovered over their bodies positioning itself above the entrance.

"The minute we step outside, he'll kill us," said Mack bluntly.

"No shit," grunted Deon, "Any ideas?"

"What do you mean? There's no way out of this we are fucked plain and simple," answered Dennis bluntly.

"There's no need for that kind of language," said Siobhan sternly.

"I think we have more important things to worry about than swearing," said Simon.

"We needn't worry the Lord will protect us," Siobhan replied.

Suddenly, the helicopter exploded in a loud bright cacophonous that crashed to the ground, exploding on contact with the earth. Instinctively, Simon and the others covered their faces from the blast. Upon seeing the smoldering wreckage of the helicopter, Simon, Dennis, Deon and Mack looked at Siobhan quizzically.

"I told you," said Siobhan with a wry smile.

Before anyone could reply a large truck drove up to the front of the lobby. An attractive woman in a white crop top was standing through the trucks sun-roof holding an M72 LAW missile launcher in one hand as wisps of smoke wafted out of the barrel.

She removed her goggles and looked at them with a smug grin. Simon and Siobhan recognized her as Fiona Ramos from the Flying Fish Trading Company.

"Sup bitches!" barked Fiona.

"I think I'm in love," said Mack upon seeing her.

"It's probably gas," commented Deon.

"Hey!" grunted Mack.

Fiona studied them; she stopped when she recognized Siobhan.

"You!" yelled Fiona furiously as she tossed the missile launcher to the side and climbed out of the truck and ran up to Siobhan.

"I've been waiting for this, remember me bitch?" barked Fiona.

Siobhan shook her head passively, "No" answered Siobhan.

"No? No! Last time we met you knocked me out!" barked Fiona as she got in Siobhan's face.

Kenji and Ben disembarked from the truck, Simon recognized the two men from several months ago.

"Oh! Yes now I remember you, the rude Mexican woman right?" said Siobhan.

"Oh shit, this is going to get ugly," said Kenji.

"Mexican? Bitch I'm Cuban and I want a rematch!" Fiona yelled.

"I'm sorry for my mistake," said Siobhan nicely.

"Trust me, you will be!" barked Fiona as she pulled back her fist preparing to throw a punch.

Before Fiona could even strike her, Siobhan punched her once in the nose. Fiona fell to the ground in a daze clutching her bloody nose with her hand.

"Sorry…again," said Siobhan.

Ben whistled impressed.

"So are you guys our ride to the airport?" Mack asked.

"Guilty as charged," said Ben sarcastically. "Let's see, Simon and Siobhan I know you two"

"But I don't know you three," continued Ben as he pointed to Mack, Dennis and Deon.

In reality, Ben knew who they were but felt it best to act otherwise.

"We'll hand out introductions later, Deng needs medical attention," said Simon.

Ben took one look at Deng and then looked back at Simon. "Get him in the truck; are the rest of you coming?"

"Yes. They go where I go," said Deng weakly before once again lapsing into unconsciousness.

"Works for me, get in the back," Ben replied.

While they helped Deng into the truck Ben helped Fiona up. "You alright?" asked Ben.

"Yeah I'm fine, that bitch is mine," said Fiona as she wiped the blood from her nose.

"Not today, now get in the truck," said Ben.

"Yeah, yeah," said Fiona as she got in the truck grumbling in Spanish.

Ben got in the driver's seat and drove to the airport as fast as he possibly could. They arrived at the airport where Deng's private plane and a doctor were waiting for them. Simon, Siobhan and Dennis got out of the car and walked to the plane while Deon and Mack carried the semi-conscious body of Deng into the plane. As they boarded the plane, Siobhan waved goodbye to their rescuers. Fiona responded by giving Siobhan the middle finger.

Siobhan ignored her and closed the door of the plane while Simon walked into the cockpit.

"Where are we going?" asked Simon, the pilot looked up at him.

"Basilan Island" answered the pilot.

*****

Watching them in his office via satellite was a very displeased Mr. One.

"Damn, Damn Damn!" barked Mr. One upon seeing that Simon Kane was still alive.

He dialed the phone number of Mr. Zero on his cellphone. After a few rings, Mr. Zero picked up the phone.

"Yes Mr. One?" said Mr. Zero.

"We have failed to kill Simon Kane, though we did manage to capture Mai Yunao" Mr. One explained nervously.

"I know I'm on my way to interrogate her now," answered Mr. Zero.

Mr. One was not surprised that Mr. Zero knew about the failure to kill Simon Kane. However, he was surprised that he was personally going to talk to Mai.

"What about Simon Kane then?" asked Mr. One.

"Mr. One, the primary goal of this operation was to humble the Triad, with that accomplished we can now deal with the Kane situation," answered Mr. Zero.

"How?" asked Mr. One.

"Don't worry about it, I will personally handle it from TREADWATER," said Mr. Zero before hanging up.

Mr. One shrugged, annoyed at the lack of information he had received from Mr. Zero but he knew that there was nothing he could do about it.

Chapter 8
King Of The Castle

Mai awoke in a small room; it was well furnished with a closet and a bathroom off to the side. There was a metal table with a lamp in the center of the room and two metal chairs. Next to the closet was a full body mirror on the wall. She was surprised at how well-furnished the room was especially since this wasn't the first time she was kidnapped. She got out of the bed and immediately noticed that she was still wearing her nightgown.

She noticed that her glasses were on the table; she walked over to the closet and opened it. Inside was white dress shirt, underwear, shoes, blue jeans and an expensive looking black cheongsam dress. Feeling chilly and somewhat exposed Mai hastily put on the clothes. Feeling slightly more comfortable, she studied her environment more thoroughly. She noticed that the bed, chairs and table were bolted to the floor.

The room was also devoid of any windows which made Mai feel even more nervous. Next to the bed was a door that led to a bathroom, while on the other side of the room was a locked door. Because she couldn't open it she knew it was the entrance to the room. Mai sat on the bed and buried her head in her hands. It was frustrating to know that she had been kidnapped by someone else again.

To be snatched out of thin air suddenly and to awaken someplace else made her feel powerless. She began to cry when she suddenly heard the metallic sound of the door being unlocked. She looked up at the door as it began to open. Into the room walked a tall, handsome looking white man, his blonde hair was smoothed backward, he was wearing black pants, a dark red dress shirt and a black blazer with a black tie.

"Good afternoon Miss Yunao," said the man politely as he placed his hands behind his back.

"Who the hell are you? And where am I?" demanded Mai as she tried to sound threatening.

"Miss Yunao, considering your present situation it would be wise to strongly monitor your tone," said the man in a soft yet menacing voice. "Now then, in answer to your question: You are now a prisoner of the Networc, as for my name you may call me....Jonas."

"So what happens to me now?" asked Mai as she tried desperately to hide the fear in her voice.

"Miss Yunao, there is no need to be nervous you will be treated well as our prisoner until our goals are met," answered Jonas.

"It's kind of hard to not be nervous when you've been kidnapped," said Mai sarcastically.

Jonas grinned at her sarcasm. "Fair enough, though I recommend that you try anyway."

"Thanks for the advice, though I won't be staying here long enough to need it," said Mai bravely.

"Oh? And why's that?" asked Jonas curiously. "Ah, I know why!" he said snapping his fingers in mock realization.

"You are referring to your father and Simon Kane right?" said Jonas smugly.

Mai said nothing even though she knew he was right.

"Miss Yunao, your father and the Triad are...indisposed at the moment thanks to our efforts," said Jonas.

"And Simon?" Mai asked.

"I'm sorry to say but Mr. Kane and his gang of reprobates are not long for this world," said Jonas. He turned away from Mai towards the door; he opened it and began to walk out. Before walking out of the room he looked back at Mai.

"Before I leave Miss Yunao know this: No one is coming for you, not your father, not Simon Kane, no one," said Jonas as he closed the door and locked it behind him.

He placed his ear against it and listened for several seconds until he heard the sound of crying. He smiled as he pulled away from the door. He turned to face his two bodyguards, Miss Hai and Lo, who had been waiting for him outside the room.

"How did it go in there, Mr. Zero?" Miss Hai asked.

"Excellent Miss Hai, everything is going according to plan," answered Jonas smugly.

"Miss Lo, is the Doctor ready?" said Jonas.

"Yes, Sir" answered Miss Lo.

"Excellent, let's go see him" said Jonas.

He turned to walk toward the elevator as Miss Hai and Miss Lo followed behind him.

Chapter 9
The Boss of Bosses

Upon arriving at a small private airfield on Basilan island, Simon, Mack, Dennis, Deon and Siobhan were greeted by a group of Triad guards and a doctor on the runway. Behind them were two black SUV's, the guards were carrying assault rifles. The doctor walked into the plane with two of the soldiers and carried Deng's limp unconscious body into one of the SUV's. The remaining soldiers beckoned to Simon and the others to get into the other SUV. Upon entering the car they were each handed a black cloth and instructed to put it over their heads by the driver.

They shrugged and put them on, the driver started the car and drove for what felt like an hour. All they could hear as the car drove was the sound of their own breathing. It was disorienting for them to be stripped of their sight. Simon had a good guess of who they were going to meet but was not completely sure.

Finally, the car stopped and the driver told them to remove the hoods. They took them off and got out of the car. They were surprised to find that they were in an underground parking garage. The driver got out of the car and walked around to the trunk at the back and opened it. He pulled out a medium sized plastic crate.

"Put your weapons in here" said the driver brusquely.

"Will we get them back?" Mack asked sarcastically.

The driver answered him with a surly look.

"I wouldn't mess with the man" replied Deon as he placed his Beretta in the crate.

"Just asking," replied Mack dismissively as he put his Tanfoglio in the crate.

Simon removed his wrist blade and Jericho and put them in the crate. The driver scowled at him, Simon sighed and removed the snub nose revolver from his ankle holster. Siobhan pulled out a Glock that she had taken off one of their attackers back on Sankan and put it in the crate as well. The guard looked at the guns in the crate and then back at them. He gestured to one of the soldiers, he gave the man the crate and said some words in Mandarin Chinese and the soldier walked away with the crate.

The driver looked back at them, "Follow me," said the driver.

Simon and the others followed him to a door on the side of the parking garage. The driver opened the door and walked through with Simon and the others following him down a ramp. At the bottom of the ramp was a hallway with doors on each side. They followed the driver to a door at the end of the hallway.

"He is in there waiting for you," said the driver as he held the door open for them.

"Thanks," said Simon as he and the others walked through the door.

"He who?" Mack asked rhetorically.

"What's your problem?" Dennis asked.

"I don't like this," replied Mack.

The room was a medium-sized space with bleacher seats on one side, in front of the bleacher seats was a small stage with a computer screen on the wall and a podium on it. Simon and Deon sat in the first row, Mack and Dennis sat in the row behind them, while Siobhan sat in the top row. Standing at the podium was an elderly Chinese man in a black suit. Simon recognized him immediately as the man who first brought him into the Triad after he left Silhouette.

"It's been a while Lin," said Simon, the man looked at him.

"Yes it has Mr. Kane. All of you take your seats," replied the old man.

"For those of you who don't know me, my name is Lin Yunao," said Lin.

"I am the leader or Mountain Master of the Heise She Li Triad," said Lin.

"What about Deng?" Siobhan asked.

"Mr. Shen is being taken to a doctor of ours where he will recover from his wounds in safety," answered Lin. "As for the rest of you, you will be receiving orders directly from me…at least for the foreseeable future."

Lin could tell what the next question to be asked was and decided to preemptively answer it. "As for our location, you are currently in a Triad safe house."

"All of this because Sankan was attacked?" asked Dennis surprised.

"Oh no Mr. Faraday, it's much worse than that," said Lin.

Lin picked a small remote off the podium and pointed it at the computer screen behind him. He pressed a button and a map of the world appeared on the screen, there were red dots on various cities across the world including Sankan. "Each of these red dots represents a major facility of ours," he explained.

"As Sankan was being attacked each of these outposts was attacked simultaneously by well-armed commando forces," said Lin. "While I was in Seoul at a meeting they almost killed me which is why I fled here immediately as part of a contingency plan"

Mack whistled impressed, "there's only one organization on the planet capable of doing something like this simultaneously," Deon said.

"The Networc," answered Simon.

"Exactly, however we have a much larger problem," said Lin.

"Simon, after you and Mai returned from Egypt I sent her into hiding," said Lin. "Somehow the Networc found out where she was and they kidnapped her,"

The words hit Simon like a sledgehammer, another woman he loved was once again in peril because of the Networc and he could do nothing about it. He punched his palm out of anger. "So…what now?" asked Simon.

"Now?" asked Lin quizzically. "Now we retaliate," said Lin bravely though Simon could tell he was just as worried about Mai as he was.

"How? From what I know of the Networc they're impossible to track," said Dennis.

"Ordinarily you would be right, however Mr. Faraday, the Networc has finally made a crucial mistake," said Lin. "You see we managed to capture one of the Networcs assassins."

"After some….persuasion, he told us some very interesting things," continued Lin.

"Like?" asked Mack.

"Like the location of a Networc agent named Counselor Morgenstern," answered Lin.

"Where?" Simon asked.

"Pripyat, he's going to be overseeing an arms deal with some Chechen terrorists," answered Lin.

"Where the hell is Pripyat?" Deon asked.

"City in Chernobyl," answered Mack.

"You sound like you've been there?" said Deon.

Mack looked up at him, "nah, I knew that from Call of Duty."

"So let me guess what the plan is," said Simon. Simon and Deon sat in the first row, Mack and Dennis sat in the row behind them, while Siobhan sat in the top row. "You want us to go into a war zone, intercept the arms deal then "talk" to this Morgenstern guy about your daughter right?" asked Simon.

"Perceptive as ever Mr. Kane," replied Lin.

"Makes sense actually," said Deon.

"How?" asked Dennis.

"Pripyat's been abandoned for decades making it secluded...and the buildings would be an excellent place to hide a sniper. My only question would be the war with the Russians," answered Deon.

"The Ukrainians are occupied elsewhere and any forces there should be minimal given the recent gains Ukraine has made," Lin explained.

"It's a trap," said Siobhan. The others looked up at her, surprised to hear her speak.

"She's got a point," said Mack.

"And Morgenstern is the bait," Simon continued dryly.

"Regardless, we have no other leads on them," said Lin.

"So just to be sure, you're sending us into a radioactive ghost town in the middle of a war to make someone tell us where your daughter is being held?" asked Mack.

"Basically, yes" replied Lin casually.

"Great, because I just wanted to know if I'd be able to cross visit Chernobyl off my bucket list," said Mack sarcastically.

"You have a bucket list?" asked Dennis.

"You don't?" Mack replied.

"Anyway, your flight to Ukraine is leaving in a few hours, so I suggest you prepare yourselves," said Lin.

Chapter 10

Run Interference

Located below the city of Moscow is the headquarters of the most secretive organization in the Russian government: The black ops intelligence agency known only as Red Curtain. Accessible only by a cold war era subway train system codenamed: Metro 2. The train system consisted of several sphere-shaped train cars that traveled to various secret entrance points around Moscow all of which led to Red Curtain's headquarters. Red Curtain itself was formed in 1941 after the Nazi invasion of Russia. Originally under the control of the Red Army it was placed under the control of the KGB in 1954.

The agency was deactivated in 1991 after the fall of the Soviet Union. However, it was reactivated in 2001 as a division of the KGB's successor known as the Foreign Intelligence

Service (SVR). The current leader of the agency, a man known as Mikhail Vorga, sat in his office far below the bustling streets of Russia's capitol city. After a few minutes two of his operatives walked into his office. Their names were Lev Khrueshenada, codename: AMPERSAND, and his partner Zoya Vladimera, codename: FIREBALL.

Khrueshenada was an older man in his mid-fifties in excellent physical shape. Khrueshenada was wearing a gray trench coat and pants with a white dress shirt and a black loose tie, his black hair had streaks of gray on the sides. His partner, Zoya Vladimera, was an attractive, much younger woman in a black leather dress jacket, a gray shirt beneath, black miniskirt with black knee-high boots and long red hair. Despite their appearances, the two of them were among Red Curtains top agents. They had been nicknamed the Gruesome Twosome by their fellow agents.

"Have a seat," said Vorga.

The two of them sat in the chairs in front of Vorga's desk. "Do either of you remember Simon Kane and Deon Bowman?" asked Vorga.

"The one-eyed American from Silhouette?" replied Lev.

"What about them?" asked Zoya.

"Ever since they left Silhouette we've been keeping track of them," said Vorga.

"Over the last several months, they have been spotted working with the Triad on Sankan Island," continued Vorga.

"Two weeks ago we spotted them breaking into a research facility in Iceland with the aid of the Devil Woman, a guild member and one other unidentified individual" said Vorga.

"I thought the Devil Woman was supposed to be dead?" Khrueshenada asked, confused.

"So did we, until she appeared seemingly out of nowhere in July," explained Vorga.

"Several hours ago, they were spotted boarding a passenger plane at Zamboanga airport in Basilan," said Vorga.

"Where are they going?" Zoya asked.

"Ukraine," answered Vorga.

Zoya and Lev sighed, ever since the war started Red Curtain had been kept out of it. The feeling among agents was that they would eventually be deployed to the war zone. However, Lev and Zoya didn't expect to be sent there for this. Vorga could sense their unease about being sent to the war zone. "I have been trying to keep us out of the war, but this is a separate matter," explained Vorga.

"What are the Americans doing about it?" asked Lev.

"Nothing, for some reason Silhouette is dragging their feet on this, and these two rogue assets could present a potential danger to our interests in the region," Vorga answered.

"Could they be attempting to join the Ukrainian military?" asked Lev.

"We are not sure, but it's possible," Vorga answered.

"So do you want us to intercept and kill them?" asked Zoya.

Vorga nodded in answer.

"What about the other three you mentioned?" inquired Lev.

"Prosecute them as needed but your targets are Simon Kane and Deon Bowman, understood?" asked Vorga.

"Yes sir" answered Lev and Zoya in unison.

"Good a plane is waiting for you at Sheremetyevo," replied Vorga as he handed Lev two file folders with information on Kane and Deon. "The plane will take you to Warsaw Chopin Airport in Poland where you will board a plane to Boryspil."

They shrugged at the instructions knowing that the war was the reason why they couldn't fly directly to Ukraine. The gruesome twosome stood up and walked out of the office. They went down a myriad of hallways till they arrived at the subway train that took them to the exit and entry point of Metro 2.

"So which one do you want?" asked Lev as the train car began to move.

"Bowman," answered Zoya, Lev handed her the folder on Bowman.

"I never thought Simon and Deon would go rogue" Zoya observed.

"That's the harsh truth of this life, you never truly know anyone," said Lev. "It's better to not get close to anyone."

"What about you and me?" asked Zoya smugly.

Lev looked at her, she had been his partner for almost three years. In that time a special bond had formed between them that neither of them could ignore. "Well, not too close," replied Lev with a sly smile.

"That's what I thought," said Zoya laughing softly.

The train stopped and they disembarked from the train and walked toward a door at the other end of the platform. They pushed a button on the wall next to the door and it opened. They stepped into the small chamber and slowly the room rose in the air and when it opened again, they were standing in a bathroom in the Bolshoi theatre. Quietly, they walked out of the theatre where they hailed a taxi for the airport.

*****

Despite her captivity, Mai was not bored in her cell. The guards would bring her books and magazines to pass the time. Every time a guard would come to her she would ask them where she was only to be given silence as a reply. She heard a loud knock on the door. She got up to answer it expecting another guard to bring her dinner however instead of the usual stone faced soldier in military fatigues she was greeted by Jonas. Behind him was a chef pushing a cart with two steaks on it.

"I figured you could use something different for diner," said Jonas politely.

He walked in and sat down at the table, the chef following behind him with the cart. Confused but admittedly hungry, Mai sat down across from him at the table. The chef placed the plates on the table in front of them. Upon studying the plate she noticed there was more than just a steak on it, there were also green beans, a roll and mashed potatoes. Mai had to admit the food smelled delicious. Jonas thanked the chef and he walked out of the cell with the cart.

"Is there a reason why you're not eating?" Jonas asked.

"Maybe, because you kidnapped me," answered Mai.

Jonas grinned subtly, "That's fair, though I assure you that your food has not been tampered with in any way," replied Jonas. "I see you don't believe me, very well, I'll demonstrate."

He stood up and walked over to Mai. He picked up her plastic knife and fork and cut off a small piece of steak and ate it. "Like I told you, nothing," said Jonas as he returned to his chair.

Mai shrugged, she began cutting into the steak and eating a bite. It tasted as good as it smelled. She looked up at him. "Why are you doing this, I'm not going to tell you anything about my father or the Triad," said Mai sternly.

Jonas laughed loudly, "Forgive me for laughing, Miss Yunao, but do you honestly think that I give a damn about your father and his fellow gangsters?" said Jonas. "If I wanted it, I could have my people make you tell me your entire life story," he continued.

"Then why haven't you done that? Why this dinner?" Mai asked.

"Simple Miss Yunao," said Jonas as he finished eating.

"Because no one ever caught a fish by treating their bait poorly," answered Jonas.

"Besides, I'll be undergoing surgery tomorrow and I thought dinner with a beautiful woman would alleviate the nervousness," continued Jonas patronizingly.

"So all I am is bait then?" continued Mai.

"No, you're also a terrible dinner guest" said Jonas.

"Why are you doing this?" asked Mai.

"You see, your boyfriend, Mr. Kane, has interfered with our plans three times this year," said Jonas. "Each time he cost us a lot of money and upset our best-laid plans"

"So why not just kill him?" asked Mai.

"Because Miss Yunao he must learn the price of interfering with our activities and I'm curious," answered Jonas.

"It doesn't' matter, he'll rescue me and stop you," said Mai defiantly.

Jonas laughed softly, "I'm sure you think he's some invincible hero."

"But the truth is, he isn't invincible, he has a weakness," continued Jonas. "And once identified, an opponent's weakness can be leveraged and exploited."

"Your saying I'm his weakness?" asked Mai.

"Exactly, Simon Kane will come for you and when he comes here to rescue you he will fail," said Jonas casually. "And he will find that there is a price to be paid for involving himself in our affairs."

Mai was silent for a minute as she listened to his words echo in her head. "And what happens to me after he learns his lesson?"

"We'll see won't we?" said Jonas as he drank from his glass of wine.

"You're insane," said Mai.

Jonas looked up at her a stern, almost insulted look in his eyes. "My dear, Jeffrey Dahmer was insane. Adolf Hitler was insane, I am not insane I am merely a businessman making a tactical business solution."

"Is that what you call it? Simon told me what you people have done, terrorism, murder and worse," said Mai.

"Of course he would say that, everyone is the hero of their own story and every story must have a villain, Miss Yunao," replied Jonas.

"I'm sure you think I'm some kind of monster" asked Jonas. "The truth is without the Networc the world as you know it could not exist"

Before he could finish speaking his phone began to ring. "My apologies," said Jonas as he pulled it out of his pocket and answered it in Korean.

After half a second of talking he returned the phone to his pocket.

"Alas Miss Yunao, I'll have to cut our dinner short, duty calls and all that," said Jonas amiably as he stood up.

He walked to the door and opened it. Before he walked out of the cell he looked back at Mai, "I'll see you later Miss Yunao" said Jonas before walking out of the cell and closed the door behind him.

Standing outside the door were Miss Hai and Miss Lo.

"Yes ladies" asked Jonas.

"Simon Kane and his compatriots just arrived in Ukraine," Miss Lo answered.

"Excellent, and the Counselors?" asked Jonas.

"They've just arrived also" answered Miss Hai.

"We've also received word that Russian Intelligence has sent a hit squad to kill Simon and Deon," said Miss Lo.

"That is…unexpected," said Jonas.

"What do you want us to do?" asked Miss Hai.

"For now nothing, but keep them under heavy surveillance and keep me abreast of the situation," answered Jonas.

"Yes Sir," replied Miss Hai and Miss Lo in unison.

Chapter 11

When Falls the Curtain

Simon, Deon, Mack, Dennis and Siobhan disembarked from the plane via the sky bridge at Boryspil airport in Ukraine. The airport had recently been retaken by Ukrainian forces and was reopened. Crowds of people were waiting for planes to take them out of Ukraine where they could escape the war.

"I miss the private jet," muttered Mack as they joined the other passengers in crossing the sky bridge.

In the airports food court, Lev sat at a table pretending to read a newspaper. Occasionally he would glance up at the gate to see if his quarry had arrived yet. Suddenly, he spotted them casually walking out of the gate. Calmly he placed the paper on the table and pulled out his cellphone. He sent a text to Zoya, notifying her that they had arrived. He returned the phone to his pocket and followed them to baggage claim, making sure to not follow them too closely lest they spot him.

Zoya was waiting in a rented car, in the first floor of the airport parking garage. She sat in the driver's seat passing the time with her phone. Suddenly she received a text marked AMPERSAND that read they're here. Zoya returned the phone to her pocket and started the car. She pulled out of the parking garage and drove to the arrivals section where she would meet Lev.

As they recovered their luggage, which consisted mostly of knives and their sidearms, Simon couldn't help but feel like someone was watching them.

"What's up, Simon?" asked Deon recognizing the look in his eye.

"I feel like we're being watched," Dennis replied.

"Dude, we're walking through an airport with a nun, and a guy with an eye patch, of course, people are watching us," said Mack bluntly. "No offense Siobhan."

"None taken," replied Siobhan softly.

"Everyone stay sharp," said Simon.

Having gotten their bags they walked to the parking lot where a car was waiting for them. "So what's the plan, we just drive to Pripyat?" Dennis asked.

"Pretty much," replied Deon.

"Great," muttered Dennis disapprovingly.

"What's the matter Dennis, you don't like radioactive ghost towns?" asked Mack.

"Not really, I also don't like radiation sickness," replied Dennis sarcastically.

"Where's the pick up?" Dennis asked as they waited at the arrivals curb.

"It'll be here," said Simon.

"Yeah, but when though?" said Dennis.

As if in answer a large black SUV pulled up in front of them. "Seriously? An SUV? I thought we were going to Chernobyl not soccer practice," said Mack upon seeing the car.

The driver, a young Chinese man, got out and walked up to Simon. "Your car Mr. Kane, compliments of the Mountain Master," said the man as he handed Simon the keys.

"Send him my regards," replied Simon.

"I will, your equipment is in a hidden panel in the trunk," replied the young driver.

"Good luck, by the way there is a surprise for you under the back seat" said the driver, as he turned and walked into the airport.

"Wonder what it is?" Dennis asked.

Simon opened the trunk and put his case inside then got in the driver's seat and started the car. Siobhan, Mack, Dennis and Deon quickly put their luggage in the back. Deon sat next to Simon, while Mack, Dennis and Siobhan got in the back seat. Once they were all inside Simon pulled out of the curb and drove away from the airport. As Simon and his team were getting in the car, Lev waited for Zoya at the curb. She pulled up in front of him and opened the door.

"Get in...old man," said Zoya with her mischievous smile.

Lev grunted slightly annoyed at her nickname for him. "I'm not that old...little girl," he muttered dryly as he got in the car. Zoya smiled at hearing his nickname for her.

"They're getting away," said Lev as Simon began pulling out of the curb.

"Not for long," said Zoya as she pulled away from the curb and followed them.

"So how long is this drive gonna take anyway?" asked Mack.

"Four hours" answered Simon.

"Dammit" Mack groaned in annoyance.

"Theres no need for that kind of language," said Siobhan.

*****

Two hours later the sun was beginning to set. On both sides of the road was a deep forest. In the distance they could hear artillery and tanks firing. Mack, Dennis, Deon and Siobhan were asleep while Simon drove. The road was mostly empty except for a lone car following behind them in the distance. Zoya tapped Lev on the shoulder, waking him up.

"It's time," said Zoya.

"Of course it is," said Lev as he rubbed his eyes. He pressed a button on the side of his chair and it slid backward revealing a hidden compartment. Lev opened it and saw an AK-74u submachine gun with a silencer and twelve magazines of ammunition next to it. He pulled out the gun and six of the magazines then closed the compartment.

Finally, he pushed the button and the seat slid forward concealing the compartment. He quickly loaded the gun and cocked it.

"Get in close," said Lev as he lowered the window.

Suddenly Simon noticed the car approaching them quickly. As it gained speed behind them he saw a man lean out of the window holding a metal object. As the car got closer he recognized it.

"Oh shit!" said Simon suddenly realizing what was about to happen. He swerved to the side just as Lev opened fire on them.

"What the hell was that?!" barked Mack, awoken along with the others by the machine gun.

"Road rage" said Simon as the others turned around to look at the car.

"Shit, and our gears in the trunk," complained Deon.

Simon jammed his foot down on the pedal and swerved to the left just as Lev unleashed another barrage of automatic fire at them. Instinctively, they knelt their heads in a desperate attempt to avoid getting hit.

"Any ideas?" Deon asked.

"What about that surprise the driver mentioned?" said Siobhan.

"Worth a shot, Mack grab it," said Simon.

"Right," said Mack as he looked under the seat and pulled out a case. He opened it and saw a Chinese Type 56 assault rifle and four magazines inside.

"This oughta even up the odds," said Mack upon seeing the rifle.

"That's quite a surprise," said Simon as Mack quickly loaded the rifle and cocked it.

"It's my kind of surprise," said Mack as he quickly lowered the window.

Suddenly another fusillade of machine gun fire hit them from the other car.

"Dammit, they'll puncture the tires if they keep this up," said Dennis.

"Screw the tires I'm worried about getting shot!" yelled Mack as he leaned out the window.

Meanwhile, Lev quickly reloaded the machine gun, Mack aimed at the car and fired two short bursts of gun fire at it. Zoya swerved to the side, narrowly avoiding getting hit.

"Where'd they get that from?" barked Zoya. Suddenly Mack caught a glimpse of the left tire and he fired a short burst at it.

Zoya lost control of the car causing it swerve out of control and into a tree on the other side of the road. Mack whistled impressed at the shot as he got back in the car.

"Hell of a shot," observed Simon.

"You expected anything less from a Ranger?" said Mack proudly.

"You were in the Rangers?" Deon asked.

"Yep" said Mack as he put the rifle back in the case.

"I knew there was a reason I didn't like you," said Deon dryly.

"That's interesting because I don't like jarheads either," said Mack sardonically.

The two men laughed at the joke. "Shouldn't we stop and find out who they were?" asked Dennis.

"No, we've got more important things to do in Pripyat," said Simon as they drove on into the night.

Lev stepped out of the car rubbing his head and felt blood pouring out from a cut on his forehead. He glanced at the SUV disappearing in the distance. He then looked at Zoya tiredly.

"Zoya you okay?" asked Lev.

"Yeah," answered Zoya as she looked up at him.

Lev pulled out his phone and dialed the electronically scrambled phone number of Mikhail Vorga. After a few rings, he was greeted with a brusque hello in Russian.

"Sir, they escaped, we need transport," said Lev trying not to sound guilty.

"Don't worry, I'm sending a car but the mission is cancelled, return to headquarters immediately," said Vorga before hanging up.

"So?" asked Zoya.

"He's sending a car, we are to return to Moscow immediately," said Lev as he returned the phone to his pocket.

"What, why?" Zoya asked surprised.

"He didn't say. It's probably politics, it always is," grunted Lev.

"Dammit!" barked Zoya as she struck the dashboard in anger.

"My thoughts exactly," grunted Lev in a sardonic tone. "Still, they might as well as be dead already."

"What are you talking about?" Zoya asked.

"If they keep going in that direction all they'll find is death," said Lev.

Chapter 12

Fires of Ghosts Long Gone

The city of Pripyat, abandoned after the Chernobyl disaster in 1986, sat like a giant gray graveyard. Each building a gravestone to a once majestic city and what might have been. The city was surrounded in all directions by a lush forest that had reclaimed the city in the absence of man. In the distance was the reactor, covered in a solid steel arch confinement structure over the still irradiated remains of reactor No.4. On the edge of Prypyat was a small amusement park, looming over the park like the all seeing eye of God were the rusted remains of a rusting Ferris wheel. When the war began the city was once again occupied by Russian forces only for Ukraine to retake it.

The once thriving city was enveloped in the omnipresent darkness of the night. The only light came from the faint glow of the moon reflecting off rusting metal and shattered glass. The sounds, typically associated with cities were not present in the long desolate city. The only sound came from leaves rustling in the wind and the distant thunder of artillery echoing across the land. The only residents of the city were the creatures of the surrounding forest. Tonight however, the animals had company in their home.

It was easy for Simon and the others to stealthily infiltrate the city. Equipped with Geiger counters they were careful to avoid areas with lethal levels of radiation. Hidden around the park were Siobhan, Dennis, Deon and Mack ready to pounce on Morgenstern when Simon gave the signal. Mack and Deon's role would be to provide sniper fire while Siobhan would be Simons backup and Dennis would be keeping watch. Simon walked up the steps of the Ferris wheel and waited, based on what Lin had told him the meeting would be here at the amusement park tonight.

"Anyone else getting flashbacks to Call of Duty?" asked Mack over the radio.

Simon, Deon, and Dennis chuckled at the joke quietly.

"What's Call of Duty?" Siobhan asked confused.

Mack glanced at her, a look of mild shock on his face. "That's just wrong"

"Call of Duty is the McDonalds of video games," grunted Dennis.

"What's wrong with McDonalds?" Deon asked.

"I prefer Burger King. Any sign of the Chechens?" asked Simon quizzically.

"Nothing" answered Dennis dismissively.

Suddenly, in the distance they could hear the engine of a quickly approaching helicopter. "Guess they're here," said Mack over the radio.

"But who? The Chechens or Morgenstern?" asked Siobhan ominously.

"We're about to find out," said Simon as the helicopter got closer. He recognized the helicopter as a Russian Mil Mi-8 transport helicopter.

"Everyone, brace yourselves" said Simon over the radio communicator in his ear. The helicopter hovered over the patch of concrete in front of the Ferris wheel. Slowly it began to land, Simon tensed himself instinctively ready to pull out his Jericho if he had to. As the helicopters wheels touched the ground the rotors slowly stopped spinning. A door opened on the side of the helicopter and out stepped three men dressed in all black with identical faces.

Simon wasn't surprised by this since he had learned that all Networc Counselors underwent plastic surgery so as to look the same, still it was haunting to see the face of the Counselor that had killed his wife in front of him once again. "You don't look Chechen," said Simon smugly. The man in the middle smiled slightly at the comment.

"No, I suppose I look more familiar," asked the man in the middle.

"Yeah, I think I killed a few buddies of yours," answered Simon.

The man in the middle laughed. "You can cease in trying to provoke me Mr. Kane, it won't work," said the man.

Simon shrugged. "Worth a shot, so I'm guessing your Morgenstern?"

"Yes, and it's Counselor Morgenstern," answered the man in in the middle.

This is Counselor Benton and this is Counselor Stenz," said Counselor Morgenstern pointing to the men on his left and right.

"I must say, we were expecting you and your friends," said Counselor Morgenstern.

"I don't have any friends," said Simon.

"That must be very lonely," replied Morgenstern.

"And quiet, I'm guessing there never were any Chechens were there?" asked Simon.

"Very astute," Morgenstern replied sarcastically with an air of arrogance.

"Yeah, I have my moments," replied Simon with equal sarcasm. "So since this isn't an arms deal, what is it?"

"Allow me to explain, our leader wishes to speak with you personally. So he sent us to escort you to TREADWATER," said Counselor Morgenstern.

Deon shivered ever so slightly when he heard the name TREADWATER in his microphone.

"Is that so?" asked Simon smugly.

"Yes, so if you'll board the helicopter with us we'll fly to the airport where a plane is waiting for us," explained Counselor Morgenstern politely.

"And if I say no?" Simon asked.

Morgenstern smiled arrogantly. "Mr. Kane there's three of us and one of you, I hardly think you're in a position to decline."

"You know something, you guys are really bad at counting" said Simon as he snapped his fingers.

Before either of the Counselors could answer, Mack and Deon fired a bullet at the heads of Benton and Stenz, killing them on contact. Counselor Morgenstern turned around shocked when a third bullet hit him in the knee. He fell to the ground writhing in pain, he looked up and saw Simon aiming a gun at him, smoke gently wafting out of the barrel. "You were saying something about positions," said Simon as he walked up to Morgenstern.

"Looks like you do have friends after all," said Morgenstern tauntingly.

"More than you," Simon replied smugly.

"It doesn't matter you'll never find her now, we were the only people who knew where TREADWATER is you fool," laughed Morgenstern.

"Wrong. See I know exactly where TREADWATER is and I don't need you assholes to get there. By the way, I'm guessing Mr. Zero knew that already," Simon replied.

Morgenstern knew he was right the more he thought about it. The man and organization he had devoted his life to, had sent him here just to die thought Morgenstern furiously. He reached into his holster to pull out his gun so he could take Simon with him at least. However, before he could even touch the gun Simon shot him in the forehead. He returned the gun to his holster and walked to the helicopter.

"Simon what are you doing? What the hell is TREADWATER?" asked Mack over the radio.

"I'm sorry guys, but I'm not letting these bastards kill any more friends of mine," said Simon as he got in the helicopter.

"What are you talking about?" Mack asked.

"I'm saying, that I'm going to handle this on my own from now on," said Simon sternly as he started the helicopter.

"Bro, you don't have to do this," protested Deon.

"Yes I do. you know as well as I do how dangerous TREADWATER is Deon," said Simon as the helicopter rose into the air. Ignoring their protests, Simon opened the helicopter window.

"Gentlemen it's been an honor, give Lin and Deng my regards," said Simon before tossing the earpiece out the window.

The helicopter flew away from the Ferris wheel getting higher and higher, eventually it was just a blinking light in the distance. Siobhan, Dennis, Mack and Deon sat there quietly in the darkness for a few minutes, shocked at what had just happened.

"We need to call Lin and tell him asap," said Deon.

"Dennis can you track him," Siobhan asked.

"No, it's impossible without his communicator," answered Dennis sadly.

"Dammit, that stubborn bastard," grunted Deon in frustration.

"I have a question, though, what's TREADWATER," asked Mack.

"Forget about it, Dennis, call Lin, tell him to put us on the first flight to Japan," Deon said.

"Japan, why Japan?" asked Mack.

"Because we might be able to intercept him," answered Deon.

Mack decided to bring up the questions Deon avoided later. "First things first we need to get outta here, pretty soon or we'll be glowing in the dark."

"The man's got a point for once, let's go," replied Deon.

"When have I ever not had a point?" Mack asked.

"You sure you want that question answered," replied Dennis.

Siobhan sat next to them kneeling with her eyes closed and her hands clasped together.

"What are you doing?" Deon asked.

"Praying for the Lord to watch over Simon" replied Siobhan.

"Let's hope he's listening," said Mack sarcastically.

Chapter 13
The Devil Listens Also

Mr. Zero awoke to a knock on the door of his bedroom. He was still tired from the surgery that ended only a few hours ago. He looked at himself in the mirror and noticed the fresh stitches over his heart. He smiled, impressed with his own cleverness, at the grisly line on his chest. He began getting dressed when he heard another knock on the door of his bedroom. "One minute!" he yelled as he quickly put on pants and a collared shirt.

Feeling sufficiently clothed he opened the door. Standing in the doorway was Miss Hai and Miss Lo.

"Well, what is it ladies?" asked Jonas.

"We have an update on Simon Kane," Miss Hai answered.

"Really?" replied Jonas pleasantly surprised at the news.

"Yes, he's apparently taken the bait and separated from his team," answered Miss Lo.

"Interesting, that changes nothing, but it's still an interesting and unexpected development," Jonas noted. "And what about the sacrificial lambs?"

"Counselors Benton, Stenz and Morgenstern are dead," replied Miss Hai.

"Now that was expected, what about Simon Kane?" asked Jonas.

"Unknown Sir, but we believe he's coming here," Miss Lo answered.

"Good, looks like we've got him hook, line and sinker," responded Jonas.

"Mr. Zero, if I may ask why have him come here, why not have the Counselors just kill him," asked Miss Hai.

Jonas smiled smugly. "It's not an unreasonable question, but I'm afraid it's a question you don't need to know the answer too,"

"Sorry Mr. Zero" replied Miss Hai.

"Forget it," replied Jonas dismissively. "Do we know why Simon left the team?"

"No, Mr. Zero" replied Miss Lo.

"What about those Russians that were trying to kill him and Bowman?" asked Jonas.

"We believe they've returned to Moscow, at least for now," answered Miss Hai.

"I see, anything else to report?" Jonas asked.

"No sir" replied Miss Lo.

"Good, well if you'll excuse me ladies I would like to freshen up," said Jonas.

"Yes, Mr. Zero" said Miss Hai and Miss Lo at once before walking away.

Jonas closed the door and walked toward the window overlooking the TREADWATER compound and the Sea of Japan in the distance. The sky was a dark dismal grey, below him were soldiers patrolling the grounds. Jonas looked out to sea, a confident grin across his face. "It won't be long now."

*****

Having just returned from Ukraine, Lev and Zoya went straight to the Bolshoi theatre. They walked into a certain bathroom and went straight for the handicapped stall and stood in front of the tiled wall for a minute. Suddenly, yet silently, a section of wall slid backward and then to the side, revealing a set of stairs that led down. They walked down the stairs to a waiting train car. They rode it for ten minutes until it stopped at their destination.

The gruesome twosome disembarked from the train car and walked down a long hallway till they reached their destination: the office of their leader Mikhail Vorga.

They knocked on the door, and were greeted with a gruff "enter" from the other side. Zoya and Lev opened the door and sat in the chairs in front of his desk.

"You look like you have questions, Zoya" said Mikhail.

"Yes Sir," Zoya replied.

"What about you, Lev do you have questions?" asked Mikhail.

Lev answered with a shrug and a grunt indicating he couldn't care less.

"Questions...everybody has them but not everyone gets them answered," said Mikhail.

"Do we get them answered?" Zoya asked.

"Depends on the questions?" replied Mikhail.

"Why are we here instead of killing Simon Kane?" asked Lev.

"Blunt as ever Lev, very well the answer is because you accomplished it," answered Mikhail.

"What?" Asked Zoya surprised. "But we didn't kill them?"

Lev sighed having realized exactly what Mikhail was talking about.

"Your mission was not to kill him it was to scare them off," answered Mikhail.

"You see, you were ultimately supposed to scare them into heading away from Russia and you succeeded," continued Mikhail. "Our scans show Kane has left the Ukraine and is heading for Turkey while Bowman and his posse appear to be heading for Japan."

"But why didn't you tell us that in the first place?" Zoya asked.

"Because if you knew you're mission was to send a message then you wouldn't have shot to kill," answered Mikhail.

"Of course," groused Lev.

"I must admit it's certainly clever," admitted Zoya grudgingly.

"Why do this in the first place, why not just have us kill them?" asked Zoya.

"Because it also sends a message to Silhouette" answered Mikhail cryptically.

"Silhouette? How?" asked Lev.

"Silhouette has been watching them since they used to be members of Silhouette, and hopefully they've gotten the message as well," Mikhail answered.

"Which is?" asked Zoya.

"Keep your people out of Russia and by extension Ukraine or else" answered Mikhail. "Now then, you two are dismissed,"

Zoya and Lev stood up and walked out of the office and went straight to the train. Once the train started moving they felt it was safe to converse. "This is bullshit," grunted Zoya.

"Welcome to the job Zoya," Lev grunted.

"You think they got his "message," Lev?" asked Zoya as the train rocketed down the tracks.

"Probably not, they're Americans, stubborn to the point of suicidal insanity, we'll see them again," said Lev.

Zoya shrugged, knowing he was right. "So…where do you feel like going for dinner?" she asked.

Lev smiled, he thought for a minute, "Torro Grill?" replied Lev.

"Of course, what is it with you and that place?" Zoya said.

"You did ask" replied Lev dryly.

*****

As soon as Takeo Kageyama entered his office, located on the top floor of the Ronin Foundation in Tokyo, his phone began to ring. Known to the world as a private security company the Foundation was in reality a black ops branch of the Cabinet Intelligence and Research Office (CIRO). Appointed to his position by the Japanese Prime Minister, Takeo Kageyama was dressed in a gray blazer, white dress shirt with a red tie and gray pants. He shrugged, annoyed at the constant electronic buzzing of his phone depriving him of even a moments rest. He was an older man, the hair on his head having retreated to the sides of his head, his suit covered in water from the rain outside. He sat down at his desk and answered the phone.

"It's been awhile, GRASSHOPPER," said a familiar voice in Japanese on the other end of the phone referring to him by his codename.

"MONOLITH?" said Takeo surprised to hear the familiar voice of Simon Kane. "What are you calling me for and how are you still alive?"

"I need your help getting into North Korea," said Simon.

Takeo shrugged. "Fine, as a favor I'll help you in exchange for your help in dealing with a problem of ours."

The voice on the other end was silent for a few seconds, "Fine," said Simon before hanging up.

Takeo looked out the window of his office at the sprawling metropolis of Tokyo beyond it. He thought for a few minutes, he picked up his phone again and dialed the phone number of the leader of Silhouette, a man by the name of General Mark Lee Connors. After a few minutes, the phone rang and he was greeted with a hello in a strong Long Island accent.

"General Connors, this is Director Kageyama, I need an update on one of your former agents codenamed MONOLITH," said Kageyama.

The voice on the other side of the phone was quiet for a several seconds.

Depending on the kind of information, it was not uncommon for Shadow agencies like Segment 25 and Silhouette to share information as long as the agencies respective countries were allies.

"Why?" Connors asked.

"I'm curious," replied Kageyama.

"Agent MONOLITH is a rogue operative being kept under surveillance," answered Connors.

"I see, rogue Silhouette agents are usually killed right?" asked Kageyama.

"Yes, I've granted him a stay of execution since it's related to another investigation," Connors replied.

"Is he aware of this stay of execution?" asked Kageyama.

Again Connors was silent for a few seconds. "I'm sure he has his suspicions but for the most part no,"

"I see, thank you General" said Kageyama as he hung up the phone before Connors could speak again.

He placed the phone on his desk then leaned back in his chair. He replayed Connors words in his head, analyzing them carefully. Silhouette and the Ronin Foundation had a long history of working together but this was different. He smiled at the fortuitous nature of MONOLITH's phone call, since it came just when he needed it. Ordinarily, he would send his own operatives to accomplish the mission, however, he felt that MONOLITH could provide assistance due to his experience. He picked up his phone and dialed a number that belonged to a member of his agency which only the Prime Minister of Japan and the CIRO's Minister knew about. The phone rang and he was greeted with a female voice.

"LILAC this is GRASSHOPPER, get DISCUS and KINO. We have a mission," said Takeo.

"Understood," replied LILAC obediently before hanging up.

He returned the phone to his pocket and returned his gaze to the window, asking himself if he was making the right call. He brushed those thoughts aside, deciding not to dwell on the matter. Ever since he had been appointed the Director of the Ronin Foundation by the Prime Minister he was forced to live with far weightier decisions, this was just another one of them.

Chapter 14
Old Favors Never Die

Demir Adem sat in the car at the airfield outside the Turkish city of Batman. He checked his watch, his client was a ten minutes late. Ordinarily this would be grounds for charging an extra fee but considering he owed this particular client a debt for saving his life he decided to let it go. Demir was a man in his early forties, a veteran of the Turkish air force now an arms dealer and smuggler. He had dark black hair with streaks of grey in it, a black goatee and a light brown complexion.

He was dressed in his usual garb of a dark grey buttoned jacket, blue jeans and black boots. Clipped to his belt was a holster containing his sidearm, a Llama M-87. After leaving the Turkish air force he formed his own arms dealing and transportation company, which he named Emperor Eagle Services. Outside the car on the tarmac rested his pride and joy as well as the work horse of Emperor Eagle Services: a CJ27 Spartan transport plane he had affectionately dubbed the Aluminum Falcon. It was payment for an arms deal he had made with the CIA years ago.

He had spent years and plenty of money outfitting the plane with everything from weapons and armor to communications equipment. In the distance he heard a car approaching, he looked over to it and smiled, his contact was here. Demir got out of the car, just as the taxi pulled up to him. The passenger handed some money to the driver. He got out of the car, upon seeing him Demir held out his hands and smiled jovially.

"Mr. Kane! It has been too long my friend!" said Demir as he embraced Simon in a bear hug.

"Nice...to...see you too Demir," said Simon as he gasped for breath.

"I was surprised when I got your call my friend," Demir continued as he let Simon go.

"If I may ask how did you get here? Ukraine is a long way from Turkey," asked Demir.

"I stole a helicopter and flew it till it ran out of gas near the Moldovan border, after that it was easy to sneak onto a plane bound for Istanbul," answered Simon confidently.

"Impressive my friend, you told me on the phone that you need transport to Japan?" Demir asked.

"Yeah, can you do it?" replied Simon.

Demir glanced at the plane and back at Simon. "Of course I can, but there's one problem"

He shrugged, "Of course there is, how bad is it," grunted Simon.

"I can't land in Japan" replied Demir.

"What do you mean you can't land in Japan?" asked Simon annoyed and confused by the reply.

"Maybe it's because I currently have a shitload of illegal guns in this plane?" answered Demir sarcastically. "However, that doesn't mean I can't get you there?"

Before Simon could ask how, a truck drove up to the airport. When it stopped in front of them seven men jumped out of it, each of them dressed in black and brandishing an Ak-47. Their faces were covered by a black balaclava that showed only their eyes.

"Friends of yours?" asked Simon.

"Disgruntled customers from Syria," Demir answered.

"I didn't know you had disgruntled customers, you must be slipping," replied Simon sarcastically.

The men in black ran towards them, cocking their rifles and yelling in Arabic. Demir looked behind him at the plane, while Simon reached for his pistol.

"Don't, when I give the signal drop to the ground and keep your head down," said Demir.

Simon had known Demir long enough to recognize that he had a plan, so he let go of the gun but remained tense as the men surrounded them screaming for them to get on their knees. Demir reached into his pocket and felt his cellphone, he quickly pressed a series of buttons on the phone.

Before he pressed the final button, Demir yelled, "Down!"

Simon and Demir quickly fell to the ground face down. Suddenly, before anyone could react there was a barrage of loud steel and fire from behind them that mowed down the men in black. When the shooting stopped, Simon looked up and saw that all the men were lying on the ground dead. He looked behind him, and saw that hanging down from a hidden compartment, suspended from the inside of the plane via a mass of wires and steel, was an M60 machine gun with smoke billowing from its barrel. The two men stood up, Simon's eyes were locked onto the gun.

"I never slip" Demir replied smugly.

Demir looked over to Simon, about to ask the question Simon was about to ask. "I had that installed after a cluster fuck in Tibet a few months ago,"

"Radar guided M60, fires a short wide angle spray at anyone in front of it," continued Demir.

"Impressive, where'd you get it?" Simon asked.

"SOFEX," answered Demir as he pulled his phone out and aimed it at the gun. He pressed a button and the gun retracted into the plane with a soft mechanical whine.

"That's quite an erector set," replied Simon.

"I like to think of it as the Falcons claws, shall we board?" said Demir.

"You're still calling it the Aluminum Falcon?" Simon asked.

"Yes, from Star Wars, why?" responded Demir.

"Never mind, let's go," said Simon dismissively, deciding not to correct him.

The two men quickly boarded the plane, Demir sat in the cockpit with Simon seated next to him in the co-pilots chair. Demir started the engines and the planes massive propellers spun, slowly at first then faster and faster. The Aluminum Falcon began moving down the runway faster and faster until they could feel it rise into the air. Simon looked out the window as the hangar, runway and the bodies began to get smaller and smaller until finally they were invisible.

"So…explain to me how you intend to get me to Japan if you can't land there?" asked Simon.

"Simple, just parachute out of the plane once we're over Yokohama," explained Demir.

"You want me to parachute over a city?" Simon asked.

"At night, besides do you have a better idea?" replied Demir.

Simon knew he didn't but he still had reservations. "How am I supposed to avoid being detected?"

"If you look in one of the crates in the back, I'm carrying a shipment of radar invisible parachutes, use one of them," Demir answered.

"What about you?" asked Simon.

"Don't worry about me, I'll be fine, I'll just turn around and head to Seoul," said Demir.

"You've thought of everything," observed Simon.

"I always do" replied Demir smugly. "By the way, I heard you had a run in with my competition"

Simon shrugged knowing exactly what he was talking about. "It's complicated."

Demir grinned smugly. "Things with Gretchen usually are"

"I'm not mad, hell if anything, I'm jealous if she weren't the competition I'd try to bed her myself," said Demir. "Thing is though, I'm surprised you did in the first place"

"Why?" asked Simon confusedly.

"Always thought she was a lesbian" grunted Demir.

"So did I" replied Simon with a smug smile in response to Demirs insinuation. "How'd you find out about that anyway?"

"A smart businessman always keeps tabs on the competition," answered Demir.

"Right, anyway I gotta make some phone calls to my pickup," said Simon as he pulled out his cellphone.

"Very well, just remember after this my debt to you is paid," Demir replied sternly.

"Whatever you say Demir, whatever you say," said Simon.

He stood up and walked into the planes cavernous dimly lit cargo hold.

Chapter 15
Race to the Sun

"So run this by me again?" asked Mack.

"Dennis is tracking his cellphone, and he detected him at an airfield in Turkey," answered Deon.

"So where are we going?" asked Mack.

"Japan," Deon answered.

"Yeah, see that's where you lose me. If he's in Turkey why not head for Turkey?" asked Mack.

Deon sighed, "Because if I know Simon he's just going to Turkey so he can get a flight to Japan," Deon explained.

"Okay," replied Mack beckoning him to continue.

"Once he's in Japan he's going to make contact with some old...friends of ours that can get him to TREADWATER," Deon continued. "Our plan is to get there first and stop him from going into TREADWATER alone,"

"Okay now I get it, there's one more thing though," said Mack. "Why do I get the feeling you're not telling us everything?"

"What the hell are you talking about?" asked Deon.

"You know damn well what, after Iceland we all found out how dangerous it is to withhold info," Mack explained.

Siobhan stood behind Deon's chair quietly and gently placed her hand on Deon's shoulder.

"I agree with Mr. Roycewicz, I think you should tell us everything" said Siobhan softly, with a hint of sternness.

Deon looked up at her and back at Mack. "What if I don't?"

"I hate to admit it but the odds are you could kill me and Dennis, but you would not survive unscathed and that's assuming Sister Stabby Mc Stab Stab behind you doesn't kill your ass first. In addition to that you're still on this private jet which is ridiculously high up and after the fight you would not be in the best condition to bail out over the ocean," said Mack.

"Your point?" asked Deon.

"My point is that it'd be better for all of us if you just answered a few questions," said Mack.

Deon glared at them and they returned his stern glare. He knew they were right but he hoped it wouldn't come to this. "I gotta admit, I thought you were dumb as shit, turns out you're not as dumb a shit as I thought you were Mack"

"My high school English teacher said the same thing," said Mack with a sly grin.

"Fine, I'll tell you everything that you need to know," said Deon.

"Smashing," said Siobhan with a satisfied grin. She walked over to the couch and sat next to Mack while Dennis sat in the other chair.

"Well?" said Deon.

"Let's start with TREADWATER; namely what the hell is it, where the hell is it and last but not least how the hell do you and Simon know so much about it?" asked Mack. Before

Deon could answer Siobhan slapped Mack lightly on the back of his head.

"Ow!" barked Mack.

"There's no need for that language," Siobhan explained quietly.

"You were saying?" said Mack ignoring the pain on his head.

Deon had already decided to leave out the fact that he and Simon were members of Silhouette. Instead he would just say they worked for the CIA and not mention Silhouette directly. "Years ago when me and Simon were in the CIA, we and several South Korean operatives were assigned to infiltrate a secret facility the North Koreans were building on Ryo-do Island."

"On the surface the op was simple, parachute in and do some recon, however, the mission went FUBAR" said Deon. "What we thought was a simple island outpost was actually a full on fortress with a supergun capable of launching radioactive shells at Japan and South Korea," continued Deon.

"How come we didn't hear about any of this on the news?" Dennis asked.

He grinned smugly. "Beyond top secret," answered Deon. "We couldn't let the North Koreans have access to a weapon like that, so we decided to go against orders and destroy the cannon with the help of the South Koreans."

"Eventually we destroyed the cannon but it was a fight every inch of the way, ultimately Simon and me were the only ones who survived," explained Deon.

"Whoa," Mack replied.

"So TREADWATER is in North Korea?" asked Dennis.

"Yeah, it was the name of the fortress," Deon answered.

"Wait I thought TREADWATER was destroyed?" asked Mack.

"Not exactly, we destroyed the gun but the base itself is still there," Deon said.

"So Simon, and by extension us, are going to break into a North Korean fortress?" said Dennis.

"Yeah, but that's why we have to stop Simon from going in himself or he'll be killed," said Deon.

"Why is he doing this and what does the Networc have to do with this?" Mack asked.

"I don't know how the Networc is connected to TREADWATER," said Deon.

"But you know why he's going there don't you?" Mack insinuated.

"Yeah" said Deon quietly with a shrug.

"Well tell us story man, the suspense is killing me," said Mack.

"The short version is that nine months ago Simon, me and....his ex-wife were recruited back to our specific branch of the CIA for a mission," said Deon.

"Wait, Simon's ex-wife was also in the CIA?" Mack interrupted.

"Yeah. She was one of the best," said Deon.

Mack whistled in surprise. "Just when you think you've heard of everything."

"Anyway, over the course of the mission she and Simon fell for each other again only for one of the Networcs agents to kill her at the end of the mission," continued Deon. "After that he swore to get revenge on the Networc, somehow he got mixed up with the

Triad and then you guys which brings us to right now."

"So...all of this, our recruitment by Deng, breaking into Vulcan has been to help one man get revenge?" asked Dennis.

"Not revenge...justice," said Siobhan.

"You think what he's doing is right Siobhan?" Dennis asked.

"It's not revenge" replied Siobhan. "Not long ago someone once told me that those who travel the road to revenge tend to get run over. I feel that what Simon wants is justice and I can understand that"

"Pretty much," said Deon.

They were all silent for a few minutes as they let her words sink in.

"If any of you want to back out, I understand," said Deon.

Mack, Siobhan and Dennis looked at each other then back at Deon.

"After everything I've been through, I'm staying," said Dennis.

"Ditto man, I gotta see how this ends," Mack answered.

"What about you Siobhan?" asked Mack.

"If it is the Lords will then I will stay and help bring our comrade back into the light," said Siobhan. "As long as you don't call me Sister Stabby Mc Stab Stab again"

"I can't promise that" said Mack dryly.

Siobhan grunted annoyed, Deon couldn't help but feel like he was back in Silhouette with Simon and Sheila. "I guess that settles it, so let's go find that cycloptic fuck and bring him in," said Deon.

They all nodded filled with a newfound sense of purpose and vigor.

"One more question," said Mack. "How come she only slaps me when I curse but none of you?"

Chapter 16
The Problem Solver

Simon Kane looked out the window of the plane at the city of Yokohama, the lights sparkling below like stars in the night sky above. On his back was the special invisible parachute that would allow him to stealthily land in the city, his trench coat was securely buttoned for protection from the cold.

"If you're going to go, go now!" yelled Demir.

Simon shrugged as he stood up and walked to the door of the plane. He pulled open the door and was blasted in the face with wind and sound from the engines and the city below. He took a deep breath and jumped out of the plane. Simon plummeted towards the city, spreading out his arms and legs to slow down his fall. He pulled the ripcord and instantly was jerked back as his rapid descent turned into a slow almost leisurely float.

Simon looked up at the plane as it was flying farther away. He looked down at the city, and began scanning for a possible rooftop to land on. He found one and angled the parachute towards it. Slowly, inexorably he drifted down to the roof of what he assumed was an empty office building. Finally, his feet touched the hard cement of the roof, he instantly performed a parachute landing fall to minimize injury. Simon stood up and instantly disconnected the parachute from his back. He looked out at the city and back at the parachute.

"There must be easier ways to avoid customs," joked Simon in an effort to reduce the stress of his situation, a technique he learned while in Silhouette.

He looked around the roof and saw the usual air conditioning equipment but on the far edge of the roof he saw a door that led into the building. He picked up his parachute and bunched it up then opened the door. He walked down a series of steps until he reached another door, not surprisingly it was locked. He kicked the door hard and it swung open revealing a long brightly lit hallway with doors on both sides each of which had numbers on them in Japanese. Simon was glad to see that he was in an apartment building since he wouldn't have to incapacitate any guards.

Simon walked quickly toward the elevator at the end of the hall. He rode the elevator all the way down to the first floor lobby. When the doors opened Simon walked straight out of the lobby into the street. They were filled with people walking down up and down the street, faces buried in cellphones. Stealthily, Simon walked into an alley adjacent to the apartment building and found a dumpster.

He tossed the balled up parachute into the dumpster. He put his hands in his pockets deciding to keep his jacket buttoned to avoid anyone seeing his gun. He walked out of the alley, relieved to be rid of the burden of his parachute. He decided to make his way to the rendezvous point with GRASSHOPPER at the Marine Tower. He hailed a taxi and after a few minutes one stopped for him, he got in and told the driver to go straight for Marine Tower.

*****

Standing straight up from the city of Yokohama, Marine Tower loomed over the city as if it was touching the floors of heaven. At the top of it sat an observation deck, while on the towers shaft were glittering white lights. Simon's taxi pulled up to the small park at the base of the mammoth structure. He paid the man with yen that Demir had given him and the driver left. Simon glanced up at the tower then shifted his gaze around the park surrounding the tower.

He was not surprised to see that the park was empty, Simon walked over to one of the benches and sat down. A few minutes after sitting down an older man walked up behind Simon and sat next to him. He was dressed in a gray suit with a white dress shirt and a red tie, Simon recognized him immediately.

"Nice night," said the man.

"Depends on what for," replied Simon.

The two men looked at each other and grinned recognizing each other instantly.

"It's been awhile MONOLITH," said the older man.

Simon never got tired of being called by his codename from when he was in Silhouette. "I hadn't noticed GRASSHOPPER."

"I must say Simon, you took quite a risk coming here considering your rogue status," said Kageyama.

"Yeah well, you know me. I'm not one for good ideas," Simon replied dryly.

Takeo laughed softly at the humor. So, what brings you to Japan?"

"Like I said on the phone, I need to get to TREADWATER and you know how to get me there," answered Simon.

"Why did you come to us? Why not go to the NIS? The South Koreans have more experience with North Korea than us, much as I hate to admit it," asked Kageyama.

"You know why" Simon replied.

"Ah, so they still haven't forgotten the last time they worked with you," replied Kageyama.

"It's hard to forget a foul up like that," grunted Simon. "So are you going to help me or not?"

"Like I said, we'll help you in exchange for your help with one of our problems," said Kageyama.

Simon sighed in mild frustration. "I was hoping you were kidding about that,"

"Do I look like I kid MONOLITH?" asked Kageyama with a look on his face as serious as a heart attack.

"Depends on how you define kidding," replied Simon.

Kageyama glared at him unimpressed and unamused by Simons sarcasm.

Simon sighed. "So what do you want me to do?"

"I have the folder right here," said Takeo as he reached into his breast pocket.

Before Simon could respond Takeo pulled out a small aerosol bottle and sprayed it in Simon's face. "What the..." said Simon slurring his speech before losing consciousness and falling to the ground.

"Sorry about that" said Kageyama as he returned the bottle to his pocket.

He put his hand up to the earpiece radio communicator. "LILAC, KINO I have MONOLITH get him in the car now."

"Yes sir," replied LILAC.

Chapter 17
Executive Sanction

Simon Kane awoke in a large room feeling slightly groggy. As he looked around the room he saw a small stage and several chairs. On the wall above the stage was a large monitor screen. Simon tried to stand up only to find that he was handcuffed to the chair. He could tell that his wrist blade and gun were also gone.

Suddenly the door opened and into the room walked a Japanese man in a red dress shirt with a white blazer, black pants and spiky unkempt black hair. Simon recognized him as Kozo Nakamura, a former Yakuza enforcer that was arrested and released from prison and subsequently drafted into the Ronin Foundation. Kozo walked to the chair on Simon's right and sat down.

"Hey Kozo," grunted Simon still groggy.

"Hey Simon, how's things?" Kozo asked.

"Shitty," Simon answered.

"And here I thought it was just me," replied Kozo.

"I'm surprised you're still working with the Ronin Foundation," said Simon.

"You're never done paying your debt to society," answered Kozo dismissively.

Just then the doors opened again and Kageyama walked into the room heading straight for the stage. "Hey boss" said Kozo dryly.

Kageyama was followed by a tall attractive Japanese woman dressed in a gray t-shirt, pants and a blazer with sandals. She had long black hair and a sheathed katana sword on her back.

They were followed by a black haired Caucasian man in a dark blue blazer and black pants. Under his blazer he wore a white T shirt with black horizontal stripes on it. He had a pencil thin black mustache and a black French beret.

Simon recognized the woman as Ryoko Sasaki, a follower of the samurai discipline recruited into the Ronin Foundation due to her martial arts skills. However, he didn't recognize the man in blue. "Long time no see, Ryoko,"

"Hello Mr. Kane," said Ryoko with a polite customary bow.

She walked to the seat on Simons left and sat down while the man in the brown jacket sat behind him.

"Now that we're all here, let's begin" said Kageyama, sounding more like a surly high school teacher than a spymaster.

"I see you've got a new member" said Simon pointing to the man in the blue jacket seated behind him.

"Ah yes, our new recruit," said Kageyama.

"My name is Achille Renfroe," grunted the man in a thick French accent.

Upon hearing his name Simon remembered hearing about him when he was in Silhouette. According to his file Renfroe was a freelance assassin wanted by various law enforcement agencies for numerous murders using his signature weapon of razor edged Frisbee discs.

"Last I heard you were in prison," said Simon.

"I still am," Renfroe sneered.

"Lighten up Frenchie," said Kozo.

"Where'd you dig him up Kageyama?" asked Simon.

"In September Mr. Renfroe was here on his own business when he was shot and thrown into Tokyo Harbor by his targets," said Kageyama.

"I think I can figure out the rest," said Simon. "The police found him half dead, you knew who he was and drafted him into your little suicide squad here right?"

"Yes," said Achille.

"Perceptive as ever Mr. Kane," replied Kageyama. "Now then shall we get down to business?"

After hearing no voices of dissent Kageyama cleared his throat.

"Recently we have become aware of an impending attack by ISIS on Tokyo," said Kageyama.

"Oh no, Muslims I'm so scared," interrupted Kozo sarcastically.

"I'm glad you're not scared Kozo because your mission is to take them out," said Kageyama.

"Wait, what?" said Kozo surprised.

"Don't be so surprised Nakamura, he wouldn't have brought us together for anything else," said Achille. "Besides, I've learned from personal experience that ISIS is not to be taken lightly."

"What do you mean personal experience?" asked Kozo.

"I've had some run inns with them in the past," Achille answered.

"This before or after you were sent to Tadmor prison?" asked Simon.

Achille gave him an angry look, "The ice is thin where you're treading American,"

"It usually is," grunted Simon.

Suddenly Ryoko slammed her sheathed sword down on the floor loudly getting their attention. "We have more important things to discuss."

"Thank you Ryoko, we have tracked the terrorists to an abandoned office building in downtown Tokyo," said Kageyama.

He reached into his pocket and pulled out a remote, aimed it at the monitor and pressed a button. Instantly, a picture of the apartment building appeared on screen, its top two floors highlighted in yellow.

"We believe all ten terrorists have taken over the top two floors of the building," said Kageyama.

"Why is ISIS coming here in the first place?" asked Simon.

"In a few days, the U.S. President is coming here for a meeting with the Prime Minister, We believe that these ISIS members intend to try to assassinate them with a bomb," Kageyama explained. "Your mission is to infiltrate the complex and take them all out"

"Hold on, I have a question why are we handling this why not give it to the cops or something," asked Kozo.

Takeo sighed. "Because if the police were sent in, it could potentially turn into a disaster that we cannot afford to have before a major meeting with the Americans," said Kageyama.

"So in other words, politics," Kozo grunted.

Simon and Achille grinned slightly at the wisecrack while Ryoko looked on impassively.

"Call it whatever you want, you have your orders. Now get ready there's a helicopter on the roof waiting to take you there," said Kageyama gruffly.

"What about me?" Simon asked.

"I've arranged for a chopper to fly you close to Ryo-do island with a raft and supplies, help us with this and it's yours," said Kageyama.

"Wait so his reward is a chopper to North Korea?" Kozo asked confused.

"You sound jealous Kozo" said Ryoko slyly.

"Oh well, I just didn't realize that North Korea had become such a hot tourist attraction," replied Kozo dismissively.

"You can come if you want," said Simon disingenuously.

"Hell of an offer but I'm afraid I can't go, too busy living," replied Kozo sarcastically.

"You should try Syria" said Achille dryly.

"If your all quite done making your travel plans, you have a mission I suggest you get to it," said Kageyama.

"What about my stuff?" Simon asked.

"You'll find it in the armory, agent LILAC will escort you there," said Kageyama.

"Once you're done a car will come and pick you up, now I have other matters to attend to so agent LILAC you're in charge," said Kageyama as he left the stage and walked out of the room.

Ryoko pulled a pair of keys out of her pocket and removed Simon's handcuffs. "Come with me"

Achille, Simon and Kozo followed her out of the room. They walked down a hallway to a door marked ARMORY in Japanese. Next to the door was a small console, Ryoko put her hand on the console and the door slid open. They walked into a room filled with all sorts of weapons from machine guns and rocket launchers to pistols and knives. On a table was Simon's Jericho and wrist blade.

Ryoko stood against the wall her eyes locked on Kozo, Achille and Simon. Simon put his gun in the holster, then picked up his wrist blade and slid it on his right wrist.

"Didn't know you were into jewelry Simon," said Kozo smugly.

Simon flicked back his wrist and out slid the knife, "It's an acquired taste."

"Nakamura, here." said Achille.

Kozo turned around to face him. He saw that Achille was holding out his pistol: a .44 auto mag. He took the gun and put it in his shoulder holster.

"You still use that thing?" said Simon.

"I can't get over the fact that you still use that Jericho," Kozo quipped as they walked over to a cabinet containing several machine guns and assault rifles.

Kozo picked up a TEC 9 SMG and slung it over his shoulder and grabbed some ammo. Simon studied the guns in the cabinet, trying to decide which of the weapons to use. He settled on a Benelli Nova Tactical shotgun. Simon picked it up and checked it, satisfied with it he slung it over his shoulder and picked up some ammunition for it and his Jericho. Achille meanwhile approached a cabinet and slung a bandolier, containing eight razor sharp Frisbees, and slung it across his shirt.

He also picked up an Uzi submachine gun and slung it over his shoulder. Simon noticing that the only weapon Ryoko had was her sword.

"Are you seriously going in there with just a sword," said Achille with disbelief.

"She doesn't even need it" said Simon.

"What?" asked Achille.

"I've seen that woman take out several Yakuza bikers with a pair of chopsticks," said Simon.

Achille looked at Kozo for confirmation since he knew her longer.

"Seriously," Kozo answered.

"It's a skill" said Ryoko.

As Simon listened to them speak he wondered about Mack, Siobhan and the others.

Chapter 18
Eviction Notice

Simon and the three Ronin agents flew to the abandoned office building now occupied by ISIS terrorists aboard a Bell UH-1 helicopter. Outside the sun was just starting to rise, its rays just beginning to dance across the still sleeping city. Inside they were all quiet for the twenty minute flight to the building. Achille, Simon and Kozo sat listening to the music playing on the radio while Ryoko sat cross-legged on the seat, her eyes closed and her sword across her legs with her hands resting on it. There was a calm collected look on her face in stark countenance with the others.

Simon had only worked with the Ronin Foundation briefly and thus wasn't as familiar with its operatives as he would have liked to be.

"I gotta ask, what she is doing?" asked Achille.

"Meditating" Kozo answered nonchalantly. "She does it before every mission."

"Meditating?" asked Simon.

"It's got to do with her samurai bullshit or something," explained Kozo.

"I thought it was called bushido?" asked Simon.

"It is bushido," Ryoko corrected opening her eyes.

"Before she was in the Ronin Foundation Ryoko was a member of the Sasaki clan," replied Kozo.

Simon had heard rumors of the Sasaki clan from his time in Silhouette. "I thought the Sasaki clan was wiped out decades ago"

"Very few of us still survive," Ryoko grunted

"Ten seconds," yelled the pilot.

Simon and Kozo cocked their weapons while Ryoko stood up. Achille drew one of his Frisbees and held it waiting as the helicopter approached the roof. As it landed on the roof, its blades still spinning, Simon opened the door and the four of them ran out of the chopper. Once they were out, the helicopter lifted off the roof and flew away. On the other side of the roof was a door that led into the building.

They began walking cautiously towards the door when the door suddenly burst open and four terrorists carrying submachine guns ran out, aiming their guns at them. Achille threw a Frisbee at one of the terrorist's necks, decapitating him. Before Simon or Kozo could shoot the other two, Ryoko drew her sword and ran at them at an almost supernatural speed. She sliced one of the terrorist's throats with the sword. Then spun around and sliced the other terrorist's hands off.

Before the last terrorist, who was standing behind her, could fire his weapon she plunged the sword into his chest and quickly pulled it out. She looked over at Simon Achille and Kozo.

"Are you coming or not?" Ryoko asked.

"Mon Dieu," muttered Achille, shocked at what he had just seen.

"I told you she's a samurai," said Kozo.

"What about me?" said Achille, annoyed at the lack of receiving attention.

They followed Ryoko inside the building and quickly descended a short dark stairwell, aware that they had just entered the hornet's nest. When they reached the bottom of the stairwell Simon kicked open the door. The three of them ran out into an empty hallway. Suddenly gunfire erupted from the end of the hallway. Achille threw another Frisbee, this time slicing off the shooter's arm. The four of them ran behind a wall for cover, just as more attackers arrived at the other end of the hallway.

Simon leaned out from cover and fired at the shooters head with his shotgun. Suddenly two other shooters ran out from the end of the hallway. Kozo aimed his Tec 9 and fired two short bursts of automatic fire at them killing them. Achille, Simon, Kozo and Ryoko ran down the hallway which led to a larger room. When they entered the room, several of the terrorists aimed their guns at them. Ryoko ran towards them and sliced two of the terrorists across the throat in one move.

Simon slung his shotgun over his shoulder, flicked his wrist back causing his wrist blade to pop out and ran towards one of the terrorists. He stabbed the terrorist in the heart with his wrist blade. As he pulled the knife out of the man's chest he noticed one of the terrorists aiming his gun at Ryoko. Simon, with his free hand, pulled out his Jericho and fired two shots at the terrorist's head.

"MONOLITH! Look out!" yelled Kozo.

Before Simon could respond Kozo raised his TEC-9 and fired a short burst of fire at a terrorist that was about to shoot Simon.

One of the terrorists lunged at Achille, the two grappled for several minutes. Achille managed to free himself by kicking the man in the stomach.

Finally free, Achille then threw the terrorist towards the wall. Before the terrorist could do anything else Achille pulled out another Frisbee and threw it at the man's forehead killing him. The fighting over, they surveyed the destruction.

"I feel like there are more of them than GRASSHOPPER said" said Achille, annoyed.

"Shit happens," said Simon dismissively.

"Hell of a way to start the day," said Kozo dryly.

Ryoko returned her sword in its sheath, walked to the other end of the room and picked up a small briefcase. She opened the briefcase and saw the bomb inside.

"Holy shit, there actually was a bomb," said Kozo.

"I'll call Kageyama and he'll send a team to dispose of all of this," said Ryoko.

"Well then let's get out of here," Kozo suggested. The three of them walked to the nearest elevator.

Kozo called Kageyama as they rode the elevator down to the first floor. By the time they exited the building two black cars and a black van were waiting for them in front of the building. Kageyama stepped out of the car and casually approached them.

"Good job, all of you," said Kageyama.

Kageyama turned to address Simon. "I'm a man of my word, Mr. Kane."

"That car will take you to the airport, where there's a plane waiting to fly you to an airfield at Niigata, there's a helicopter and equipment waiting for you there as well," said Kageyama pointing to car.

"The pilot will take you as close as possible to TREADWATER," continued Kageyama.

"After that you're on your own," said Kageyama.

"Story of my life," grunted Simon.

He walked to the car and opened the door. Before getting inside he turned to face Takeo, Achille, Ryoko and Kozo.

"Thank you for your help, all of you," said Simon.

"Any time," said Kozo.

Simon closed the door and started the engine and drove to the airport. Achille, Takeo, Ryoko and Kozo watched as the car disappeared down the road.

"Why do I feel like this is the last time we'll be seeing him," said Kozo.

*****

The rhythmic hum of the plane's muffled engine lulled Mack and the others to sleep. They had been flying for hours, heading straight for Japan in the hope of capturing their errant leader.

"Wake up!" yelled the pilot from the cockpit.

Lethargically Deon, Siobhan, Mack and Dennis opened their eyes.

"What is it?" yelled Mack, annoyed at being woken up.

"We're changing our flight path," the pilot answered.

"What? Why?" barked Deon.

"Orders from the Mountain Master, we are rerouting to Sokcho," answered the pilot.

"Where's Sokcho?" asked Dennis still rubbing the sleep out of his eyes.

"South Korea," Mack answered.

"Gee thanks Encyclopedia Brown," muttered Dennis sarcastically.

"Is there a reason why we're going there?" asked Deon.

"Ask him when we get there" replied the pilot angrily.

"Well I guess we're going to South Korea then," said Mack dryly.

"By the way, how do you know where Sokcho is?" asked Dennis.

"I was hired to do a job there a few years ago," explained Mack.

Chapter 19
Fool's Errand

Simon glanced out the window at the ebony cloak of the night as the helicopter flew nap-of-the-earth across the Sea of Japan. The helicopter was a Kawasaki built Boeing CH-47 Chinook outfitted with stealth equipment. Simon was dressed in his dark blue trench coat, underneath it was a black shirt with his shoulder holster, and black pants. On the floor in front of him was a zodiac, an inflatable motor boat commonly used by various Special Forces units across the world. Kageyama had also provided Simon with a grappling gun, a silenced scoped M4 carbine assault rifle, flash and fragmentation grenades, ammunition and a silencer for his Jericho.

According to the pilot, the plan was to drop Simon off twenty miles from Ryo Do Island. From there he would ride the zodiac to

TREADWATER while the helicopter would turn around and return to Japan.

"We're here!" yelled the pilot.

Simon buttoned his trench coat, closed his eyes, took a deep breath and thought of Sheila. He opened them and pulled out his Jericho followed by the silencer which was in his pocket. He screwed the silencer onto the pistol and returned it to his holster as the helicopter descended towards the ocean. Simon quickly loaded his equipment into the zodiac and slung the carbine over his shoulder. The pilot opened the lowered door of the helicopter; it was a smooth ramp so the boat could be slid out.

The rotors from the helicopter kicked up the placid waters into a violent froth. Simon pushed the boat into the water, he tapped the side of the helicopter before getting into the zodiac so the pilot would know he was in it. Simon watched as the helicopter slowly rose higher and higher in the air. Simon was positive he saw the pilot wave at him as the helicopter rose. The helicopter turned around and flew back towards Japan, Simon watched it fly off into the distance until it was gone.

Simon shrugged, he yanked the cord on the boats outboard motor back. It hummed to life and the boat sped forward toward TREADWATER.

*****

Mack, Siobhan, Dennis and Deon landed at a small private airfield outside the city of Sokcho. As they disembarked from the plane, they were greeted by several Triad men in black suits standing in front of two SUV's. Siobhan, Mack, Dennis and Deon got in one of the SUV's. Once they were inside they drove away from the airport. They drove quickly through the city finally arriving at the harbor.

They pulled up to a large freighter with a stairway leading up to it. They got out of the car and followed the driver onto the boat. He led them inside through a maze of corridors. Suddenly the boat lurched forward.

"We're moving," muttered Dennis.

"Yep," said Mack.

They followed the driver through the ships labyrinthine hallways. Finally, they stopped at a door marked private. The driver opened the door and they walked into a large room. On the walls were computer screens and on the ground were various Triad personnel working on computers.

"What is this?" asked Dennis.

"Looks like mission control," replied Mack.

They followed the driver through the room to an office at the far end. The driver stopped at the door and looked at them.

"He's waiting inside," said the driver.

"Well that's not ominous at all," Mack muttered.

Deon opened the door and walked into the room followed by Mack, Dennis and Siobhan. The room was an ornate office with a window that provided a view of the main room. Seated behind a wood desk in the middle of the room was a man in a swivel chair with his back to them. In front of the desk were four leather chairs. The driver closed the door behind them as they sat down. As soon as the door closed, the chair spun around and they were somewhat surprised to see who it was.

"Lin!" said Deon upon seeing him.

He was dressed in a black suit with a black vest, a white dress shirt with a black tie and trench coat.

"Welcome to the Zheng," said Lin politely. "You're probably wondering what this is exactly?"

"It's a shipping freighter we bought from the Russians, we've converted it into a mobile command center," explained Lin smugly.

"So…why are we here and not Tokyo?" asked Mack.

"Because Simon's no longer there," Lin answered.

"What?" asked Deon surprised.

"One of our agents in Niigata spotted him boarding a helicopter at a JASDF airbase," answered Lin.

"No doubt heading for TREADWATER," said Deon.

"Exactly, upon discovering this, I flew here to personally oversee the assault," answered Lin.

"Assault?" asked Mack confused.

"On this ship is a small army of elite commandos as well as enough attack helicopters to transport them there," answered Lin.

"What kind of helicopters?" asked Mack.

"Five armored MH-6's with rocket pods and mini guns," replied Lin.

"Nice," muttered Mack impressed.

"What about Deng?" asked Siobhan.

Lin was surprised at her question.

"He is recovering at a safe house, though he sends his regards. Rest assured he is feeling better," said Lin.

Siobhan smiled faintly, pleased with the answer.

"So...why are you here at all?" Mack inquired.

"These people kidnapped my daughter, attacked my men and tried to kill me, this is personal," said Lin sternly.

"So what about Simon?" asked Deon.

"He's probably at TREADWATER already, fortunately we should be there by tomorrow evening," answered Lin.

"Then what?" asked Dennis.

"I send you in with my men to rescue Simon and my daughter," said Lin.

"Wait so we're actually invading North Korea?" said Dennis.

"Yes, but you needn't worry, Ryo-Do is an island so you won't be facing an endless wave of Korean soldiers," said Lin.

"Oh, so there's some good news," said Mack sarcastically.

"What about me?" asked Dennis. "I'm not a soldier or anything," continued Dennis.

"Mr. Faraday, we will be utilizing your talents here to help coordinate the attack," said Lin.

"Oh, good it's nice to feel useful," muttered Dennis.

"For now, I want you all to rest and prepare yourselves for the battle tomorrow," said Lin.

"Now that I can do," said Mack.

"I'm sure, my assistant will show you to each of your quarters," continued Lin.

"This is the weirdest pleasure cruise I've ever been on," muttered Mack.

*****

After an hour Simon arrived at TREADWATER, it was a massive structure on the coast. The coast was rocky and rough with waves crashing against the massive turret in front of Simon. TREADWATER looked more like a medieval fortress than a military base. It was in the shape of an octagon with a turret on each of its eight points. In the center of it was a large courtyard that served as a parking lot for tanks, helicopters and assorted equipment. Just seeing one of its turrets again brought back rough memories of the place for Simon.

He brushed those thoughts aside as he pulled out his grappling gun. He aimed it at the top of one of the turrets, aiming carefully despite the choppy sea. Seizing his moment he fired the grappling gun. Its hook shot up into the air and embedded itself into the stone of the turret. Simon tugged on to it to see how secure it was. Satisfied, he clipped it to his belt and pressed a small button on the back of it that said retract in Japanese.

With a barely audible mechanical whine the winch on the gun began to pull Simon into the air. Simon looked down just as a wave smashed his boat against the rocks. He looked back up at the turret knowing full well that he had just passed the point of no return. He swung towards the tower until his feet touched it. Using the gun he slowly walked up the side of the tower.

Finally, he reached the top of the turret; he climbed over the guardrail, and removed the grapple. He clipped the gun to his belt and looked around. Simon noticed a door to his left, he cocked his M4 and kicked it open. He looked to his left and right in case there were any guards, he sighed, relieved to see none. He walked down a set of stairs as he drew his M4 and cocked it.

As he walked down the stairs he tried to remember the layout of the facility. If Mai was anywhere she would be in the jail cells which were in this turret thought Simon. He thought about whether to find and kill Mr. Zero first or rescue Mai. He knew there was only one option, so he went straight to the jail cells upon exiting the stairwell. The base was relatively quiet since most of the guards were asleep.

Finally Simon arrived at the jail cells; they were in a long hallway with doors on both sides. Upon entering the hallway the lights immediately switched on. Simon braced himself ready for anything. Several seconds later the lights switched back on. Standing at the end were two Asian women with short black hair.

One of them was dressed in a black dress and the other in a dark red dress. Simon noticed that they were the same height with identical features.

"The hell?" muttered Simon upon seeing them.

"Welcome Mr. Kane, we have been expecting you," said the woman in the red dress.

"I am Miss Lo," said the woman in the black dress. "This is my sister Miss Hai," she continued pointing to the woman in the red dress standing next to her.

From their appearances, Simon could tell they were unarmed, so he walked toward them slowly and cautiously.

"Nice to meet you ladies, ordinarily I'd like to get to know you better, but I'm here for a friend," said Simon smugly, his finger on the trigger.

"We're sorry Mr. Kane, but our employer wishes to speak with you now," said Miss Lo as they began walking toward him.

"I'm afraid I have to say no" said Simon. He aimed the M4 at them and began firing short bursts of fire at them. To Simons surprise the two women ran towards him in a serpentine pattern. Simon fired several short bursts at them. Tracking their movements as best he could with the rifle but missing due to their speed. Before Simon knew it Miss Hai was standing in front of him.

She kicked him in the stomach so hard he went flying back across the room, dropping his rifle.

"I'm afraid we must insist," said Miss Lo, they stood in a combat stance.

Wearily Simon stood up, ignoring the pain in his chest.

"I don't usually hit women, but for you two I'm willing to make an exception," growled Simon. He snapped his wrist back causing the blade to pop out. Simon ran at them and tried to hit them with the blade. As

Miss Hai and Miss Lo ran towards him they jumped off the walls moving too fast for Simon to hit them. As they fell to the floor behind Simon, he spun around with his wrist blade hoping to hit them. With his other hand Simon threw a punch at Miss Hai but she grabbed his arm before the blow could connect with her face.

Her grip was like a vise as he desperately tried to free himself. He tried to draw his wrist blade hand hitting but before he could even raise it Miss Lo grabbed it from behind him. She held his arm against his back, Simon tried freeing himself but to no avail. Suddenly, Miss Lo struck him in the neck with the side of her left hand. Simon felt himself lose consciousness as their grips loosened he fell to the ground.

Before he lost consciousness, the last thing he saw were Miss Hai and Miss Lo standing over him.

"Shit," grunted Simon just before losing consciousness.

Chapter 20

The International Man

Simon awoke in what appeared to be an ornate dining room. He tried to stand up but noticed that his wrists were chained to the table and his ankles chained to the floor. On the back of his chair was his trench coat, he also noticed, not surprisingly, that his weapons were gone including his wrist blade. He looked around the room, in front of him was a wooden table of medium length with a chair on the other end. On the walls were gold framed portraits of Kim Jong Un, His father Kim Jong Il and his grandfather Kim Il Sung. Suddenly a man walked inside, he was a well-built white man with blonde slicked back hair, wearing long black pants, black blazer with a dark red dress shirt underneath and a black tie.

Behind him were Miss Hai and Miss Lo carrying what appeared to be plates with food. In one hand and drinks in the other. The man in the suit sat in the chair at the other end of the table. Miss Hai carefully set her plate and drink on the table in front of him, the man thanked her. Miss Lo put her plate in front of Simon, he scowled at her which she ignored. Simon looked at the plate before him, on it was a Filet Mignon steak with a side of mixed vegetables and mashed potatoes with a roll.

The drink was a brown liquid with ice in it that looked like tea, on the side of the plate was a plastic fork and knife. As delicious as the food smelled, Simon couldn't help but feel like he was being given his last meal.

"That will be all ladies," said the man politely.

Miss Hai and Miss Lo nodded and walked out of the room. The man waited until they had left and shut the door behind them. Once they were gone he slowly turned to face Simon who was more confused than ever.

"You know, there are easier ways to contact me?" said the man with a sly grin.

"I'm not one for the easy way," grunted Simon.

"Clearly," the man replied dryly.

"So what's up with the twins?" asked Simon.

"The one in the black dress is Miss Hai and the one in the red dress is Miss Lo, they're my bodyguards and personal assistants," said the man in the suit.

"I found them at an underground fighting tournament in Vietnam, I took them in and paid for them to be trained in martial arts," continued the man in the suit.

"Nice to know the names of the people who kicked my ass," said Simon sarcastically.

"They make me feel like a James Bond villain, it's quite enjoyable," replied the man.

"Don't forget what always happens to Bond villains," said Simon.

The man laughed, "I believe a proper introduction is in order."

"I already know who you are so allow me to introduce myself," continued the man. "My name is Jonas Mannheim though I believe you know me by my sobriquet, Mr. Zero."

Upon hearing that name all reason and logic fled as Simon instinctively lunged towards him stopped only by the chains on his wrists and ankles. Ignoring him, Mannheim casually picked up his fork and knife and cut off a piece of steak and ate it. "Are you done?" asked Mannheim.

Simon sat down, his reason quickly returning.

"Honestly, I could have had you killed in any number of increasingly violent and brutal ways, instead I have my personal chef make you a delicious dinner and you try to kill me? Gratitude is clearly not a specialty of yours, Mr. Kane," said Mannheim. Simon glared at him icily. "Oh come on Mr. Kane, just because you came here to kill me does not mean we cannot be civilized about this little disagreement of ours"

"Little disagreement? You bastards killed my wife!" barked Simon.

"We have killed many more than your wife, but why allow such unpleasant affairs to rob us of our sanity?" Mannheim replied.

Simon was about to speak when he realized there was nothing he could do for now. He shrugged, picked up his plastic knife, cut a piece of steak and ate it.

"It's good isn't it? Mai thought I had drugged the food, crazy right?" asked Mannheim.

Simon looked up at him the anger slowly returning. "Mai? Where is she?"

"She's fine, don't worry about it, however that could all change with a snap of my fingers," said Mannheim threateningly.

Simon realized the only way he might rescue Mai and escape from here was to keep his emotions in check.

"You know, this whole mess could have been avoided. Seriously, if you'd have just let that woman's death go we wouldn't be in this most unfortunate of situations," continued Mannheim.

"Her name was Sheila," growled Simon.

"Yeah her, if you just let it go then that would be that," Mannheim answered dismissively.

"But nooo you had to go all action hero on us and become a major pain in my ass," continued Mannheim casually waving his fork in a circle as he said the words.

"How come I'm not dead then?" Simon asked.

"The reason you're not dead Mr. Kane, is because you impressed me," answered Mannheim.

"How?" asked Simon raising his eyebrow, surprised by his answer.

"I wanted to meet the man who managed to singlehandedly derail several of our biggest plans," answered Mannheim. "After all, ever since we were formed no one has done what you have and survived an encounter, or in your case encounters, with one of our Counselors"

"Who are you people?" asked Simon as Mannheim continued eating.

Mannheim looked up at Simon and smiled. "Ahhh, now that's the real question isn't it. The question that's been gnawing at you all year"

"I can't see the harm in telling you since the odds are quite high no one will ever hear it or believe you. "I'm sure you think we're just another assortment of terrorist nut job's with a preposterous list of demands," said Mannheim.

"Pretty much yeah," replied Simon bluntly.

"Well here's the thing, you can believe that fairy tale all you want but the reality is far different," said Mannheim. "You see, we are the men who really run the world."

"And you say you're not crazy," shrugged Simon as he cut off another piece of steak.

"Touché Mr. Kane, it's true, you see the short version of our illustrious history is this," said Mannheim. "After World War Two my grandfather and seven other CEO's came to the conclusion that the world's governments are thoroughly incapable of preventing Armageddon because they are consumed by weaknesses like greed and arrogance,"

"So they decided to establish an organization that would infiltrate the world's government's and influence them towards a more positive direction," continued Manheim. "Ever since then we have used our resources to manipulate history so as to stave off disaster"

"You're insane," grunted Simon.

"Am I? Turn on the news Mr. Kane and you'll see nothing but war, rape, pestilence and lies," replied Mannheim. "Nothing is being done to stop it and the leaders of the world act more like children than leaders,"

"They are so caught up in petty politics and squabbles that they fail to prevent that which should be prevented above all else," continued Mannheim. "No Mr. Kane, we are not insane, the world is insane and we are the psychiatrists."

"So tell me how stealing nuclear weapons and trying to blow up dam's helps anyone?" Simon asked.

Mannheim smiled, "I knew you would bring that up, first in Belarus we were stealing those weapons to prevent radicals from using them,"

"And as for the dam, we were going to use its destruction to overthrow the government and install a more stable one... since every great enterprise needs capitol both financial and political," answered Mannheim.

"In a way people like you are part of the problem actually," said Mannheim.

"How?" Simon asked.

"How are you not? For example do you remember a few weeks ago when you and your cronies stole that drive from us?" replied Mannheim.

"Yeah," Simon grunted.

"Well that drive contained the location of a nuclear weapon your leaders so foolishly lost," explained Mannheim. "We were going to recover it and decommission it,"

"Sure you were," said Simon sarcastically.

"I can see that you're not convinced, Americans really are the most stubborn of people," said Mannheim as he cut off the last piece of steak.

"Speaking of which, you just implied you're not American so what are you exactly?" asked Simon.

"A good question, I was not born in any country I was born on my father's yacht in the middle of the Atlantic Ocean in international waters," answered Mannheim. "As such I am above petty things like nationalism and patriotism,"

"I like to think of myself as the International Man," continued Mannheim.

"And this setup you have here with the North Koreans is another result of your machinations?" asked Simon, gesturing to the paintings on the walls with his fork.

"Exactly, much like North Koreas nuclear weapons program, this facility was built with our help, just another in a long list of favors this country owes us," said Mannheim.

"That's quite impressive," said Simon disingenuously.

"Almost as impressive as a single man doing what no one else ever has in addition to finding us," replied Mannheim.

"I aim to please," replied Simon sarcastically.

Suddenly, Mannheim held up his hands in protest. "You know what lets shift gears for a minute."

"Have you ever read Watchmen?" asked Mannheim nonchalantly.

"What?" Simon asked looking at him, surprised at his question. *What kind of game is he playing now?*

"Watchmen. One of the greatest comic books of all time? It was made into a movie in 2009?" said Mannheim.

"Yeah, I've read it. Personally, I prefer Kingdom Come," he replied as he took a sip of tea.

"Excellent choice" replied Mannheim. "Anyway, in Watchmen do you remember why Ozymandias destroyed New York?"

"Yeah, he was trying to prevent World War Three by tricking the US and Russians into thinking aliens were attacking so they would stop antagonizing each other. Kinda dumb if you think about it," Simon answered.

Mannheim smiled softly at Simon's response as if in mockery of his answer. "Ozymandias had the right idea but it was his plan that was flawed, in fact I always thought his plan and the Networcs ultimate goal are very similar,"

"I agree that you're both insane," grunted Simon.

"Hardly," laughed Mannheim. "Like Ozymandias we are humanitarians, but also realists.

"The great powers of the world have proven themselves too inept, corrupt and self-destructive to effectively govern and any attempt at removing them from power would be met with failure and the status quo being maintained," continued Mannheim.

"Manipulating them on the other hand is quite a different endeavor," said Mannheim with a sly grin. "With the right amount of power and influence you can make anyone do anything"

"And plenty of dead bodies," Simon interrupted accusingly.

Mannheim shrugged. "Think of them as a sacrifice for tomorrow," he said dismissively.

"Like I said earlier, people are ultimately ruled by their own selfish desires and as such are unfit to govern themselves," said Mannheim. "We, of the Networc are not, we are above such trivialities and weaknesses and as such are better equipped to rule after all we have been doing it since 1946,"

"I'm not really seeing a difference between before and after," replied Simon dryly.

"And yet World War Three has yet to happen, Mr. Kane," countered Mannheim.

"Is this the part where you ask me to join you?" Simon asked sarcastically.

Mannheim laughed. "I must admit Mr. Kane having you in our ranks would be quite the benefit but in all honesty it never occurred to me. However, let me ask you a question."

"I'm not really in a position to refuse," Simon replied.

"When you were in Silhouette did you ever wonder if the missions you went on did any real good for anyone? If any of the tortures you suffered or the murders you committed contributed to a better safer world?"

Simon looked down and went silent. It was a question he had asked himself many times over the years, everyone in his line of work has. Mannheim made some good points but then he remembered seeing Sheila and cradling her body rendered lifeless by one of this man's subordinates. He remembered his vow to avenge her and the friends he made on the long road that led him here. He remembered Mai, an innocent dragged into this conflict and locked in a cell. He thought about these things and many others and knew his answer.

He looked up at Mannheim. "I won't deny it, I've asked myself those questions," replied Simon. "In my life I have witnessed acts of horrific cruelty and evil but also acts of compassion and justice from people of all walks of life."

"People are not perfect, I know that better than anyone. Your methods however strip people of their fundamental right to make their own decisions in life," continued Simon.

"Even when those decisions have shown that they often result in disaster," Mannheim asked.

"Generally speaking people are much better and smarter than you give them credit for," answered Simon.

"History says otherwise Mr. Kane," replied Mannheim.

"Letting people make mistakes that they refuse to learn from time and time again sounds especially cruel and corrupt especially when they now have the means to destroy the world several times over," he continued.

"The only cruel and corrupt person I see in here is you, in fact I have a counter offer for you," replied Simon.

"Is that so?" asked Mannheim.

"Actually yeah," said Simon with a defiant smirk. "Why don't you just lie down and die instead?"

Mannheim grinned at Simons words, looking almost entertained. The two men looked at each other quietly for several seconds. "I really don't think you want that."

"Are you sure about that?" said Simon.

"Yes I am, in fact I'm positive that my death is the last thing you want," answered Mannheim smugly.

"What are you talking about?" Simon asked.

"I knew you were coming here with the intention of killing me, so I underwent a certain...surgical procedure in advance," said Mannheim.

"What kind of surgical procedure?" Simon asked.

"I had a doctor implant a device in my heart, while two of my operatives planted two bombs of considerable power in two of the world's largest cities, one bomb for each city" answered Mannheim.

"I can tell by the look on your face that you've already figured it out, if my heart stops beating for even a second the device in my heart will cause those two bombs to detonate taking many lives in the process," said Mannheim with a smile, convinced that he had just won.

"You're lying," said Simon in disbelief.

"Maybe I am, maybe I'm not but can you really take that chance?" asked Mannheim.

"Assuming you're not lying, where are they?" asked Simon.

Mannheim casually shrugged his shoulders, "I don't know, one of them could be in New York the other could be in London...or Tel Aviv or Beijing"

"Hell one of them could even be in your hometown of Long Branch, New Jersey," said Mannheim. "What I do know is that they are in places with lots of people and they are very well hidden"

Simon glared at him as he clenched the fork in his hand.

"Besides, even if I did know where they were, do you really think I would tell you?" asked Mannheim.

"Did you really think I would accept your offer?" Simon answered sarcastically.

"Touché, so in a nutshell, if you did make good on your promise to kill me you would be responsible for the deaths of hundreds maybe even thousands," said Mannheim. "So the real question is: how badly do you want revenge?"

Simon sat at the table, trying to think of something to say.

"You know what? I'll let you rethink my offer and digest what I've said, In the meantime I'll think of a way to convince you to see things my way," said Mannheim.

Before Simon could respond, two North Korean soldiers walked into the room. One of them restrained Simon while the other unchained him. Once he was free he tried to struggle free, in response one of the guards kicked him hard in his stomach with his knee. He fell to his knees clutching his stomach, as one of the soldiers brought the butt of his rifle down on the back of his head knocking him unconscious.

The two guards looked at Mannheim for orders. "Take him back to his cell gentlemen" said Mannheim as he raised his glass to them.

The two guards nodded and dragged him out of the dining room.

Chapter 21
Crimson and Clover

The guards brought Simon to the cells, they stopped at a cell door on the far end of the dimly lit hallway. One of them opened the door, once the door was open the guards roughly tossed Simon into the cell and quickly closed the door behind him and locked it.

"Simon?" said a voice in front of him, a voice he hadn't heard in a long time.

He looked up and was surprised to see, sitting up on a bed looking just as surprised to see him was Mai Yunao.

"What are you doing here?" she asked incredulously.

"I took a wrong turn at Albuquerque," said Simon sarcastically.

He tried to stand up but stumbled a little, before he knew it Mai was standing next to him helping him up. "It's alright, I'm fine," protested Simon as he walked to the bed and sat down.

Mai sat next to him as he buried his face in his hands and took a deep breath. "So...you came here to rescue me didn't you?"

"Yeah that's me, your goddamn knight in shining armor," grunted Simon.

He looked up at her finally getting a good look at her, she was just as beautiful as Simon remembered. She was wearing a white tank top and underwear, her long black hair was down, her black glasses made her look like a librarian. Simon noticed two bulges on her arms that weren't there the last time he saw her. She noticed him gaze at her arms and shrugged shyly.

"I've been exercising since we last saw each other," said Mai.

"I never would have figured you for a workout freak," said Simon with a smile.

Mai shrugged, "it's mostly push-ups and a few sit ups," she replied sheepishly.

"Are you ok?" asked Simon.

"Yeah, I'm fine, what about you?" asked Mai.

"I've felt worse," replied Simon trying not to think about his conversation with Mannheim.

"I'll bet, remember when you rescued me on Sankan?" said Mai.

"Yeah, I still have the scar from the bullet," said Simon, as he remembered when he first met Mai.

It was three months after Sheila's death, when he had been recruited by the Triad to rescue her from the clutches of the Rojas Cartel. After he rescued her, he became her bodyguard for six months while the Triad assembled his team. Initially, Simon and Mai had a somewhat antagonistic relationship. However, as they spent more time together they developed feelings for each other, feelings that they had yet to sort out.

"So what's your plan for escape?" Mai asked.

"Don't have one" he answered bluntly.

"What?" asked Mai surprised.

"I got nothing" said Simon, hating to admit it.

"We'll think of something" said Mai confidently. "Still, I missed you,"

Simon smiled, "so did I,"

"It's funny, I was thinking the other day about that night in Tangier," said Mai as she looked up at him.

Simon thought for a minute then smiled as he remembered it. "Yeah, it was...quite a night,"

"For both of us," said Mai.

As they spoke their eyes met and they slowly began moving closer to each other. They both knew what was on each other's minds and they didn't care. Gently Mai removed her glasses as their faces moved closer. It was as if there was nothing else in the world but them. Suddenly they kissed each other and embraced each other in passion.

"This is crazy, doing this in a jail cell," said Mai as Simon began kissing her neck softly.

"Yes, it's absolutely certifiable," said Simon as they held each other.

Mai took off her shirt, while Simon took off his, as they held each other again caressing each other's bodies. Their hearts were racing as they quickly undressed. Mai lay down on her back with Simon on top of her, they looked at each other. The events of the past few days no longer mattered to them, just each other.

"I should've come to Korea sooner," said Simon with a sly grin.

Mai smiled, "shut up" said Mai coquettishly as she grabbed him by his neck and gently pulled him down to kiss him.

Chapter 22
All to Play For

Deon, Mack, Dennis and Siobhan walked into the cargo hold of the Zheng. The room was the size of a football field and crowded with dozens of Triad soldiers preparing for the attack. In the center of the cargo hold, next to each other were the MH-6 helicopters. The helicopters were accompanied by pilots and mechanics making the final adjustments to them. A half hour ago Lin had notified the crew via intercom that they were within range of Ryo Do Island.

On the ground in front of each helicopter was a blue tarp with the rifles for the assault teams. Siobhan, Mack, Dennis and Deon approached one of the helicopters. Siobhan, Mack and Deon smiled, pleased to see that their preferred weapons were included. Mack picked up his pistol and put it in the holster under his Hawaiian shirt. Then he picked up an FN SCAR assault rifle. Siobhan picked up two M1911 pistols and put them in her shoulder holsters, then picked up an M16 assault rifle.

Deon picked up an M9 Beretta pistol and put it in his belt holster then picked up a scoped M14 sniper rifle. While they examined their weapons and got some ammunition, Dennis studied the helicopter.

"Looks kind of delicate," said Dennis.

"Looks can be deceiving," said a cocky voice from the other side of the helicopter.

Before Dennis could respond, a young Chinese man in a dark green flight suit with short spiky black hair and aviator sunglasses walked out from the other side of the helicopter. On top of his flight suit was a brown leather flight jacket. Deon, Mack and Siobhan noticed a bulge under his arm, they reasoned it was a pistol. He approached Dennis with the casual swagger common to pilots.

"All of these helicopters have been modified so they can shrug off anything stronger than a direct hit from an RPG," said the man.

"I see, and you are?" replied Dennis.

"Yi Yaozu they call me Sky King, I'm your pilot," answered the man as he and Deon shook hands.

"You any good?" asked Deon dryly.

Yi smirked cockily realizing he was being sized up. "With a name like Sky King what do you think?" he replied sarcastically.

"I've noticed that everyone here looks ex-military?" said Mack.

"I've noticed that too actually" said Deon as he slung his rifle over his shoulder.

"Wow nothing gets past you Americans does it?" said Yi. "Yeah all of us are ex-MSS and PLA Special Forces, most of us were recruited from South Blade by the Mountain Master"

"Me personally, I used to be in the PLAAF," said Yi.

"Why'd you leave?" asked Deon.

"We didn't leave we were fired, what about you three?" Yi asked.

"U.S. Marines," replied Deon.

"Rangers," Mack answered.

"IRA," said Siobhan.

"What about him?" asked Yi, pointing to Dennis.

"Me? Oh…um tech support." replied Dennis feeling like an idiot.

Yi looked at him for a minute and laughed. "Now I've seen everything,"

"Anyway, we'll be taking off any minute now," continued Yi.

"How?" asked Dennis as he pointed to the ceiling.

Suddenly a loud alarm sounded above them followed by the sound of metal scraping against metal above them. Siobhan, Dennis, Deon and Mack looked up and saw the ceiling sliding apart to the sides revealing the sky and drenching the hold in sunlight.

"That answer your question," said Yi smugly.

"Dude," said Mack impressed.

As soon as the roof had finished sliding to the side the other soldiers and pilots boarded their helicopters. One by one their engines roared to life and the rotors began to spin.

"That's our cue," said Yi as he got into the helicopters cockpit. Mack and Siobhan grabbed their rifles while Deon climbed inside.

Mack and Siobhan joined him in the helicopter and strapped themselves in as Yi started the engine. Slowly they began to rise in the air careful so as to avoid a collision with the other choppers.

"Good luck guys!" yelled Dennis.

Mack looked down at him and gave him a thumbs up with his left hand.

They joined the other helicopters above the ship and followed them in a tight formation towards Ryo Do. "You know something just occurred to me?" said Mack suddenly.

Deon and Siobhan looked at him, a curious look on their faces.

"What?" asked Deon.

"It'll take us an hour to get there, we need some music," answered Mack.

"Don't worry about it" said Yi, he pressed a button on the console and instantly Paranoid by Black Sabbath began playing on the speakers above them.

"That's what I'm talking about" said Mack. As they flew farther away from the ship Deon, Mack and Siobhan began slowly nodding their heads to the music.

Chapter 23
Devil's Ultimatum

Simon and Mai's sleep was interrupted as six North Korean guards barged into their cell. Behind them were Miss Hai and Miss Lo. They aimed their Ak-47 rifles at them, surrounding them and demanded they get dressed. Simon and Mai got out of bed and put on their clothes. Simon put on his black shirt, and green pants while Mai put on her white tank top, blue jeans and glasses. One of the soldiers walked towards Simon holding his trench coat in his hand.

Simon was surprised that he got it back in the first place and put it on.

"We get imprisoned in North Korea and that ugly thing still survives," said Mai sarcastically.

"Shut up!" barked one of the soldiers in Korean as he raised his hand to hit her.

Before the blow could connect Simon caught it with his hand. "I wouldn't," growled Simon as he gripped the man's arm tightly.

In response the other soldiers aimed their rifles at him, before they could pull the triggers Miss Hi told them to stop in Korean. The men lowered their rifles, Miss Lo turned to face Simon and told Simon to let him go.

Simon complied and the man scowled at him. Miss Hi walked into the room with three soldiers and ordered them to place a black bag over Mai's head and her hands in cuffs.

"What the hell are you doing? Let her go!" barked Simon.

They ignored him as Miss Hi motioned for them to bring Mai with them. Simon followed them out of the room and was about to try to help her when Miss Lo kicked him in the back of his left knee causing him to fall to his knees. Before he knew it she had a knife to his throat and was kneeling behind him.

"Move and you never see her again, understand?" whispered Miss Lo quietly as he watched Mai disappear into the hallway.

Simon nodded and stood back up and scowled at the impassive face of Miss Lo as he rubbed his neck. She motioned to the remaining three soldiers who obediently grabbed him from behind and placed a bag over his head and cuffs on his hands. As they escorted him out of the cell Simon wondered what Mannheim had planned for him now.

When the bag was taken off Simon saw he was in the courtyard in the middle of the base. He was standing on a metal platform with a small staircase leading down to the courtyard with a railing on the left and right of the staircase that went around the platform. Miss Hai and Lo were standing behind him while Mannheim stood in front of him, with his back to him. Usually at this time of day, the courtyard would be filled with soldier's going about their daily tasks. However, the courtyard was devoid of all save for a few vehicles and one solitary wooden pole in the center of the courtyard.

Mannheim turned to greet him, "Good morning Mr. Kane," said Mannheim as he motioned to Miss Hi to remove his handcuffs.

Obediently Miss Hi reached into her pocket, pulled out a key and removed Simon's cuffs.

"Where's Mai?" Simon demanded.

"In a minute, we have much to discuss," Mannheim answered cryptically.

He reached into his pocket and pulled out Simon's armband containing his retractable wrist blade.

"Starting with this," said Mannheim as he held it up in front of Simon. "This is quite a little gadget, we found it when we were searching you for weapons, I almost cut my finger playing with it"

"Too bad it wasn't your neck," said Simon.

"Lose the attitude Mr. Kane, what's yours is mine and what's mine is…also mine," said Mannheim.

Simon glared at him in response. "That was a joke, I was trying to be funny" said Mannheim. He sighed. "So much for levity."

He glanced behind Simon to Miss Hai and Miss Lo. "You two want this?" asked Mannheim as he held up the armband.

"I'll take it," said Miss Lo.

"Here, it's yours" replied Mannheim dismissively as he tossed it to her.

She caught it in her right hand and put it on her left hand.

"What can I say, Asians love knives, no offense ladies," said Mannheim as he glanced at Miss Hai and Miss Lo.

"Anyway back to business," said Mannheim as he turned back to face Simon. He reached into his pocket and pulled out a walkie-talkie. "Gentlemen, if you would," said Mannheim in Korean.

Immediately four soldiers walked out of the base, in between them was a young woman with a bag over her head. Simon knew instantly that it was Mai.

"What are you doing?" Simon growled.

"You'll see," said Mannheim dismissively.

He watched in horror as they tied her to the pole in the center of the courtyard. Then the guards turned and walked several paces away from the pole and drew their rifles. Simon suddenly realized what they were getting ready to do. He was about to grab Mannheim when he heard the unmistakable sound of a gun being cocked. Simon glanced to his left and saw Miss Hai aiming his Jericho at his head, its silencer removed. Simon stepped back.

"Now that we've dispensed with the histrionics, let's get down to business," said Mannheim.

Simon nodded reluctantly, his eye locked on Mai, his mind trying to think of some way to save her.

"I was thinking about our talk last night, about human nature, specifically your theory that people aren't completely morally bankrupt sheep," answered Mannheim. "It's an interesting theory, and like all interesting theories, it must be tested."

"And then it hit me!" he said with an excited snap of his fingers.

"There is nothing in this world you want more than my death which, if that happens will cause those bombs to go off killing a considerable amount of people, but you will have avenged what's her name," continued Mannheim.

He put his hands behind his back and glanced at Miss Hai as if he was about to address her. "Miss Hai if you would?" ordered Mannheim.

Miss Hai nodded and aimed the pistol at Mannheim's temple. *What the hell?* Thought Simon.

"Those soldiers will shoot Miss Yunao in five minutes unless I say otherwise," said Mannheim.

"But if you say stop, she will be spared and you will both be allowed to leave, however, if you don't Miss Hai will shoot me in the head triggering the bombs and you get your revenge," said Mannheim.

"So Mr. Kane, what is more important: revenge or her life? Just be advised the clock is ticking," asked Mannheim with a devilish grin.

Chapter 24
Moment of Truth

"You're insane," said Simon.

"Mr. Kane, once again I'm not insane and the clock is ticking," replied Mannheim tapping his watch tauntingly.

Simon realized that it would be pointless to try and reason with him. He thought, not about Mannheim's ultimatum but how to escape with Mai.

"How many innocent lives is your revenge worth?" said Mannheim tauntingly.

Ignoring Mannheim, Simon couldn't think of a possible way to escape.

"Do it, Mr. Kane prove me right show me that you care more about revenge then her," continued Mannheim.

"You have three minutes left Mr. Kane, prove that deep down you're just as evil and useless as everyone else and that the world needs us!" yelled Mannheim, a sadistic smile across his face.

The two men stood there silently waiting for the other to say or do something as time seemed to move slower and slower.

"Tick tock tick tock, Mr. Kane," said Mannheim as sweat began to appear on Simon's forehead.

Suddenly, the silence was interrupted by an explosion from above and a subsequent cascade of rock and metal. They looked up and saw that the top of one of the towers had erupted and was now consumed in fire and smoke. The explosion was followed by the sound of an engine that was getting closer. Just then six helicopters flew overhead strafing the fortress with rockets and machine gun fire.

"Deus ex machina bitches!" yelled a familiar voice from one of the helicopters.

A voice that Simon didn't expect to hear again: the voice of Mack Roycewicz. The North Korean soldiers, in front of Mai scattered, aimed their rifles at the choppers and began firing. Immediately the other soldiers began firing at the helicopters from the fortress, while others ran out into the courtyard.

"Well...I didn't see that coming," said Mannheim as he looked on watching the helicopters above attacking the fortress.

Simon noticed Miss Hai and Miss Lo weren't paying attention.

Taking advantage of their momentary distraction, Simon quickly hit Miss Hai in the stomach as hard as he could with his left elbow. She stumbled backwards and dropped the gun. Simon spun around and punched Miss Lo as hard as he could in her face knocking her to the ground. He quickly knelt down and picked up the Jericho, and retrieved his wrist blade from the unconscious body of Miss Lo.

"Thanks for holding my stuff for me," growled Simon.

Before he could even cock the pistol, Miss Hai grabbed him by the back of his trench coat and threw him over the railing. Simon landed on his back, his pistol had fallen next to him. Simon looked up behind him and saw that Mannheim was running through the door into the fortress. As he approached the door he turned to face him and smiled that arrogant smile Simon despised.

"We'll talk again Mr. Kane," yelled Mannheim before opening the door and disappearing into the castle.

He turned around and saw that Miss Hai and Miss Lo had already disappeared behind him. Simon grabbed his pistol and stood up intending to run after him, but then he remembered Mai standing in the middle of the courtyard still handcuffed to the pole.

He looked over at her and was relieved to see she was still alive, struggling to free herself amidst the chaos. Simon knew what he had to do. Up above, Deon was picking off various North Korean soldiers that were shooting at them from the fortress walls and the courtyard.

"Yi! You've got to get us down on the ground!" yelled Deon.

"I'm trying!" barked Yi. "I'm a little busy at the moment!"

Mack was firing at the North Korean soldiers in the courtyard when he saw something unexpected.

"Guys look! Its Simon!" yelled Mack pointing to a figure running across the courtyard.

"Crazy mother fucker!" barked Deon upon seeing him. "Siobhan lower the rope!"

Siobhan lowered the rope so they could rappel down to the courtyard. They climbed down it as fast as they could one by one while Deon provided covering fire from the helicopter.

Simon ran as fast as he could when he was suddenly knocked to the side on the ground. He looked up feeling dazed, and saw a North Korean soldier aiming a gun at him. Before he knew what had happened, the back of the soldiers head exploded and the guard fell to the ground next to him. Behind him was Siobhan holding an M16 with smoke wafting out of the barrel. She lowered the rifle, smiled and waved at him. Not knowing what else to do, Simon waved back at her.

Suddenly Siobhan swung around and began firing at the heads of various North Koreans, her aim switching from one to the other methodically. Mack ran over to Simon and helped him get up.

"Dude, you okay?" Mack asked.

"Could be better, what the hell are you doing here?" asked Simon.

"You really think we were going to let you have all the fun," replied Mack.

Simon ignored him as he looked over at Mai. To his horror, she had stopped struggling and was now lying still, blood pouring from the side of her forehead.

"Cover me," said Simon before running toward Mai.

"What?" said Mack as he saw who Simon was running towards.

"Holy Shit!" said Mack as he followed Simon.

As Simon ran toward her he couldn't help seeing images of Sheila's lifeless body in front of him again. Mack ran as fast as he could following Simon to Mai. Behind him were three charging North Koreans firing at them. Mack turned around and fired a short three round burst at their heads with his SCAR. As they fell he glanced over at Siobhan. She was firing at several charging soldiers when suddenly her gun jammed.

Undeterred, she threw the M16 at one of the soldiers knocking him on the ground. One of them tried grabbing her from behind while several other soldiers ran towards her. Siobhan snapped her head backward causing the man who grabbed her to stumble backward clutching his now bloody nose. Siobhan grabbed the knife hanging from his belt and plunged it into his neck. She then turned around and threw the knife at one of the other attacking soldiers, hitting him in the stomach.

She pulled out her .45 colts, one in each hand, and began firing at them.

Mack looked up at Deon in the helicopter firing at various attacking North Korean commandos. He looked back over at Simon and noticed that a soldier was aiming a pistol at his head. Mack quickly aimed his SCAR at the man's hand and fired. The gun fell from the man's hand, just as Simon saw him. Simon swung around and fired two bullets at the man's head killing him instantly.

He turned and continued running towards Mai with Mack following him.

As Mack watched Deon, Simon and Siobhan in action an idea began to occur to him that he decided to brush aside for now. As Simon ran toward Mai he saw two guards run in front of him. He quickly aimed his pistol at the two men and shot them before running past them. Simon arrived at Mai's lifeless form as she hung limply from the pole. He was relieved to see that her head had just been grazed by a bullet, rendering her unconscious.

Simon used the butt of his Jericho to break the chain links connecting the handcuffs. He held Mai in his arms trying to wake her up.

"She okay?" asked Mack, upon seeing her.

"She's fine, listen I need you to get her on that helicopter and then get the hell out of here," said Simon sternly.

"You got it, but what about you?" replied Mack.

"I've got a score to settle," said Simon.

He turned and ran towards the platform. Simon kicked open the door, Mannheim had disappeared into, and ran inside. Mack waved to Yi in the helicopter and pointed to Mai frantically. Yi saw Mack waving at him, holding an unconscious woman in his arms. He looked closely at her, suddenly realizing who she was.

He immediately brought the helicopter down while the other helicopters covered them. Mack and Siobhan ran to the helicopter and put Mai inside first.

"Get in we are leaving!" yelled Yi.

"What? But Simon?" asked Deon.

"We have to go now, this was only meant to be a rescue mission, if we don't leave now we're dead, the air force has been mobilized," yelled Yi.

Deon, Mack and Siobhan hated to admit it but he was right, they knew that those planes could easily down the helicopters in one pass. Once Mack and Siobhan got inside, Yi signaled the other helicopters that they had Mai and began to take off. The other helicopters provided cover for them as they flew away from TREADWATER.

*****

Mannheim entered the boathouse at the bottom of the fortress on the other side. In the middle of it was a small speedboat in the water ready to take him to safety. He was about to get in when he heard the click of a gun being cocked behind him. Mannheim sighed in annoyance and slowly turned around to see Simon aiming his pistol at him.

"I've made my decision," said Simon.

"Really? Mr. Kane, be reasonable you're not going to kill me. You're far too loyal to your ideals to kill me," said Mannheim smugly.

"See here's the thing about that," said Simon as he holstered his pistol.

Before Mannheim could respond Simon punched him in the nose as hard as he could. Mannheim stumbled backward before falling on his back. Instinctively, he put his hand to his nose and noticed his blood trickling out of it. He looked up at Simon dumbfounded by what had happened.

"What the hell are you doing? You can't kill me you fool?" stammered Mannheim.

"I never said I was going to kill you. As we speak Mai is on a helicopter flying to safety," said Simon. "Which means you've lost one of your bargaining chips genius," he continued as he slowly walked towards Mannheim.

For the first time Simon saw a look of pure fear on Mannheim's face, the mere sight of it made everything he had gone through seem worth it.

"But the bombs?" protested Mannheim.

"Like I said, I'm not going to kill you," said Simon. "But that doesn't mean I can't make you pay for what you did," he said looking down at Mannheim.

"What are you going to do to me if you can't kill me?" asked Mannheim.

"Give you something to remember me by," said Simon as he cracked his knuckles.

Suddenly, Simon brought his left foot down hard on Mannheim's left knee. The action was followed by a loud crack drowned out by a scream of intense pain from Mannheim. Simon did the same to Mannheim's right knee with his right foot producing the same results. He did the same to Mannheim's left and right arms again causing screams of anguished pain to come forth from Mannheim.

Simon knelt down, "I've just broken your arms and legs, you'll heal assuming you get out of here alive," said Simon. "Which I'm sure you will,"

"You will pay for this," stammered Mannheim weakly as he tried to ignore the pain.

"Probably, but you're going to have to find me first, so tick tock," said Simon as he pulled out his pistol.

Simon struck him in the face with the butt of the gun, rendering him unconscious.

Simon checked his heartbeat, pleased that it was still beating. He walked away from Mannheim's body towards the boat. He was pleased to see that the keys were already in the ignition. He turned the keys and the boats engine roared to life.

He stepped on the acceleration and piloted the boat out of the boat house at ever increasing speed. He looked behind him and saw fires and smoke billowing forth from the TREADWATER compound. In front of him far in the distance, he could see faint images of six helicopters flying away deeper into the Sea of Japan. He smiled, secure in the knowledge that Mai was safe. He looked at the GPS console on the dashboard of the boat.

On it was a map of his location, in the north was the Russian city of Zarubino. Simon turned the boat in the direction of the city and drove there at full speed.

Chapter 25

Services Rendered

Lin Yunao sat at his desk in his office on the Zheng, in front of him were four envelopes on his desk. Casually he checked his watch, any minute now he expected four very angry people to barge into his office. The helicopters had returned to the Zheng, he had been informed that his daughter had been hit and was being taken to the ships infirmary. He planned to go see her as soon as his business with her rescuers had been concluded. Suddenly the door to his office flung open, into the room walked Deon, Siobhan, Dennis and Mack. Much to his surprise none of them began insulting him.

"Have a seat, all of you, we have much to discuss," said Lin.

"You got that right," said Deon as the four sat down in the seats in front of his desk.

"Let's cut right to the chase," said Lin. "First, thank you all for saving my daughter."

"I owe you a lifelong debt for saving her," continued Lin.

"Then give us a helicopter and send us back for Simon," said Deon bluntly.

Lin sighed, "regretfully, that is neither possible nor wise," answered Lin. "For one, the North Korean military has locked down that facility making it impossible for anyone to get in there and second well...he's no longer there."

"What do you mean he's no longer there?" asked Mack dumbfounded.

"I didn't stutter did I? In case I did allow me to repeat myself: He. Is. No. Longer. There" replied Lin, annoyed at having to repeat himself.

"How do you know?" asked Mack.

"Shortly before you left for the island I had Mr. Faraday hack into a Minute Broadcasting satellite," answered Lin. "We used that satellite to keep an eye on TREADWATER."

"While you were flying back here, we detected a small speedboat leaving the compound heading straight for the Russian city of Zarubino," continued Lin.

Siobhan, Mack and Deon looked at Dennis curiously.

"This true?" asked Deon.

"Uh huh" Dennis replied.

"Obviously, we can't be sure it's him but if anyone could escape from TREADWATER it would be him," said Lin. "If you intend to go after him, I won't stop you since you are no longer employed by the Triad."

He picked up the four envelopes on his desk, "these envelopes contain your payment for helping us," said Lin.

Mack picked up one of the envelopes, opened it and was stunned by the amount on the check inside. "Are you serious?" he said looking back at Lin.

"Quite, you all performed admirably so you therefore get paid the full amount...plus a little extra considering what happened to Simon," said Lin.

Dennis and Deon picked up their envelopes while Siobhan didn't.

"Miss Costello? Your check?" said Lin.

"Donate it to a charity, I don't need it" Siobhan answered.

"As you wish" said Lin, Siobhan, Dennis, Mack and Deon stood up and shook hands with Lin then walked out of the office.

"So what now?" asked Mack as they closed the door behind them.

"What do you mean? It's over" replied Dennis.

"I don't know about the rest of you but I'm going to go look for Simon," said Deon.

"Good for you, but what are the three of us supposed to do?" asked Mack.

"He does have a point," said Siobhan.

"See, she gets it," said Mack.

"I can tell you have an idea, so spill it," Deon replied.

"Over the last couple of weeks we've become a hell of a team so why throw that all away?" said Mack.

"What are you saying?" Deon inquired.

"I'm saying we find Simon and convince him to join us" said Mack.

"Join what?" asked Deon confused.

"Anybody here ever see the A-Team?" answered Mack with a smile.

Dennis and Deon smiled, as they realized what Mack was suggesting.

"What the hell, I'm in," said Deon.

"I got nowhere else to go, so yeah I'm in," replied Dennis.

"What about you Siobhan?" Mack asked.

They looked at her curious as to her answer. Siobhan smiled and looked up at them. "I believe the Lord brought us together for a reason so yes I'm in," she answered.

Deon, Mack and Dennis all smiled, pleased with her answer.

"I have a question though," said Siobhan.

"What?" asked Mack speaking for Deon and Dennis.

"The T.V. show or the movie?" asked Siobhan.

A score is settled in Book eight of the Shadow World Series: Live to Die Twice...

Thank you for reading Vengeance is Forever
Please post a review on Amazon

Check out other books in the
Shadow World Series

Sanction Blue
Edge of the Abyss
Hell to Pay
Death Dealers Incorporated
No One Lives Forever
Never Say Forever